"*Are you offended because you're not my type?*"

Violet blushed furiously. "I think we've already established that you're not my type either!" She bristled. "And shall we just move on?"

"Is your

"I really

"And er
isn't go

Violet's
approp
mouth
took he
her sta
hers wa
most se
all she
could d

All about the author...
Cathy Williams

CATHY WILLIAMS was born in the West Indies and has been writing Harlequin® romances for some fifteen years. She is a great believer in the power of perseverance, as she had never written anything before (apart from school essays a lifetime ago!), and from the starting point of zero has now fulfilled her ambition to pursue this most enjoyable of careers. She would encourage any would-be writer to have faith and go for it! She lives in the beautiful Warwickshire countryside with her husband and three children, Charlotte, Olivia and Emma. When not writing she is hard-pressed to find a moment's free time in between the millions of household chores, not to mention being a one-woman taxi service for her daughters' never-ending social lives. She derives inspiration from the hot, lazy, tropical island of Trinidad (where she was born), from the peaceful countryside of middle England and, of course, from her many friends, who are a rich source of plots and are particularly garrulous when it comes to describing Harlequin Presents® heroes. It would seem, from their complaints, that tall, dark and charismatic men are way too few and far between. Her hope is to continue writing romance fiction, providing those eternal tales of love for which, she feels, we all strive.

Other titles by Cathy Williams available in ebook:

A DEAL WITH DI CAPUA
THE SECRET CASELLA BABY
THE NOTORIOUS GABRIEL DIAZ
THE SECRET SINCLAIR

Cathy Williams

—

His Temporary Mistress

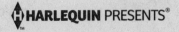

3 1218 00468 8934

Recycling programs
for this product may
not exist in your area.

ISBN-13: 978-0-373-13212-6

HIS TEMPORARY MISTRESS

First North American Publication 2014

Copyright © 2014 by Cathy Williams

This edition published by arrangement with Harlequin Books S.A.

For questions and comments about the quality of this book,
please contact us at CustomerService@Harlequin.com.

® and TM are trademarks of Harlequin Enterprises Limited or its
corporate affiliates. Trademarks indicated with ® are registered in the
United States Patent and Trademark Office, the Canadian Trade Marks
Office and in other countries.

Printed in U.S.A.

His Temporary Mistress

To my three daughters, Charlotte, Olivia and Emma, and their continuing support in all my endeavors...

CHAPTER ONE

So IT WAS bad news. The worst possible. Damien swivelled his leather chair so that it was facing the magnificent floor-to-ceiling panes of glass that afforded his office suite such spectacular views of London's skyline.

The truism that money couldn't buy everything had come home to roost. His mother had been given the swift and unforgiving diagnosis of cancer and there was nothing a single penny of his bottomless billions could do to alter that bald fact.

He wasn't a man who ever dealt in *if onlys*. Regret was a wasted emotion. It solved nothing and his motto had always been that for every problem there was a solution. Upwards and onwards was what got a person through life.

However, now, a series of *what ifs* slammed into him with the deadly precision of a heat-guided missile. His mother's health had not been good for over a year and he had taken her word for it when she had vaguely told him that yes, she had been to see her GP, that there was nothing to worry about…that engines in old cars tended to be a little unreliable.

What if, instead of skimming the surface of those assurances, he had chosen to probe deeper? To insist on bringing her to London, where she could have had the best possible

medical advice, instead of relying on the uncharted terri-
tory of the doctors in deepest Devon?

Would the cancer now attacking her have been halted in
its tracks? Would he not have just got off the phone to the
consultant having been told that the prognosis was hazy?
That they would have to go in to see how far it had spread?

Yes, she was in London now, after complicated arrangements and a great deal of anxiety, but what if she had come
to London sooner?

He stood up and paced restlessly through his office,
barely glancing at the magnificent piece of art on the wall,
which had cost a small fortune. For once in his life, guilt,
which had been nibbling at the edges of his conscience for
some time, blossomed into a full-scale attack. He strode
through to his secretary, told her to hold all his calls and
allowed himself the rare and unwelcome inconvenience of
giving in to a bout of savage and frustrating introspection.

The only thing his mother had ever wanted for him had
been marriage, stability, a good woman.

Yes, she had tolerated the women she had met over the
years, on those occasions when she had come up to London to see him, and he had opted to ignore her growing
disappointment with the lifestyle he had chosen for himself. His father had died eight years previously, leaving
behind a company that had been teetering precariously
on the brink of collapse.

Damien had been one hundred per cent committed to
running the business he had inherited. Breaking it up, putting it back together in more creative ways. He had inte-
grated his own vastly successful computer firm with his
father's outdated transport company and the marriage had
been an outstanding success but it had required consider-
able skill. When had he had the time to be concerned over
lifestyle choices? At the age of twenty-three, a thousand

years ago or so it seemed, he had attempted to make one serious lifestyle choice with a woman and that had spectacularly crashed and burned. What was the problem if, from then onwards, his choices had not been to his mother's liking? Wasn't time on his side when it came to dealing with that situation?

Now, faced with the possibility that his mother might not have long to live, he was forced to concede that the single-minded ambition and ferocious drive that had taken him to the top, that had safeguarded the essential financial cushion his mother deserved and required, had also placed him in the unpalatable situation of having disappointed her.

And what could he do about it? Nothing.

Damien looked up as his secretary poked her head around the door. With anyone else, he wouldn't have had to voice his displeasure at being interrupted, not when he had specifically issued orders that he was not to be disturbed. With Martha Hall, the usual ground rules didn't work. He had inherited her from his father and, at the age of sixty-odd, she was as good as a family member.

'I realise you told me not to bother you, son...'

Damien stifled a groan. He had long ago given up on telling her that the term of affection was inappropriate. In addition to working for his father, she had spent many a night babysitting him.

'But you promised that you'd let me know what that consultant chap said about your mother...' Her face was creased with concern. She radiated anxiety from every pore of her tall, angular body.

'Not good.' He tried to soften the tone of his voice but found that he couldn't. He raked restless fingers through his dark hair and paused to stand in front of her. She would have easily been five ten, but he towered over her, six foot four of pure muscular strength. The fine fabric of his hand-tailored charcoal trousers and the pristine white of his shirt lovingly sheathed the lean, powerful lines of a man who could turn heads from streets away.

'The cancer might be more widespread than they originally feared. She's going to have a battery of tests and then surgery to consolidate their findings. After that, they'll discuss the appropriate treatment.'

Martha whipped out a handkerchief which she had stored in the sleeve of her blouse and dabbed her eyes. 'Poor Eleanor. She must be scared stiff.'

'She's coping.'

'And what about Dominic?'

The name hung in the air between them, an accusatory reminder of why his mother was so frantic with worry, so upset that she was ill and he, Damien, was still free, single and unattached, still playing the field with a series of beautiful but spectacularly unsuitable airheads, still, in her eyes, ill equipped to handle the responsibility that would one day be his.

'I shall go down and see him.'

Most people would have taken the hint at the abrupt tone of his voice. Most people would have backed away from pursuing a conversation he patently did not want to pursue. Most people were not Martha Hall.

'So have you considered what will happen to him should your mother's condition be worse than expected? I can see from your face that you don't want to talk about this, honey, but you can't hide from it either.'

'I'm not hiding from anything,' Damien enunciated with great forbearance.

'Well, I'll leave you to ponder that, shall I? I'll pop in and see your mother when I leave work.'

Damien attempted a smile.

'Oh, and there's something else.'

'I can't think what,' Damien muttered under his breath as he inclined his head to one side and prayed that there wouldn't be a further attack on his already overwrought conscience.

'There's a Miss Drew downstairs insisting on seeing you. Would you like me to show her up?'

Damien stilled. The little matter of Phillipa Drew was just something else on his plate, but at least this was something he would be able to sort out. Had it not been for the emergency with his mother, it would have been sorted out by now, but...

'Show her up.'

Martha knew nothing of Phillipa Drew. Why would she? Phillipa Drew worked in the bowels of IT, the place where creativity was at its height and the skills of his highly talented programmers were tested to the limit. As a lowly secretary to the head of the department, *he* had not been aware of her existence until, a week previously, a series of company infringements had come to light and the trails had all led back to her.

The department head had had the sternest possible warning, meetings had been called, everyone had had to stand up and be counted. Sensitive material could not be stolen, forwarded to competitors... The process of questioning had been rigorous and, eventually, Damien had concluded that the woman had acted without assistance from any other member of staff.

But he hadn't followed up on the case. The patent on the software had limited the damage but punishment would have to be duly meted out. He had had a preliminary interview with the woman but it had been rushed, just long enough for her to be escorted out of the building with a price on her head. He had more time now.

After a stressful ten days, culminating in the phone

call with his mother's consultant, Damien could think of
a no more satisfying way of venting than by doling out
just deserts to someone who had stolen from his company
and could have cost millions in lost profits.

He returned to his chair and gave his mind over completely to the matter in hand.

Jail, of course. An example would have to be set.

He thought back to his brief interview with the woman,
the way she had sobbed, begged and then, when neither
appeared to have been working, offered herself to him as
a last resort.

His mouth curled in distaste at the recollection. She
might have been a five foot ten blonde but he had found
the cheap, ugly working of the situation repulsive.

He was in the perfect mood to inform her, in a leisurely
and thorough fashion, that the rigours of the British jus-
tice system would be waiting for her. He was in the perfect
mood to unleash the full force of his frustration and stress
on the truly deserving head of a petty criminal who had
had the temerity to think that she could steal from him.

He pulled up all the evidence of her ill-conceived attempts at company fraud on his computer and then relaxed
back in his chair to wait for her.

Downstairs, in the posh lobby of the most scarily impressive building she had ever entered, Violet waited for
Damien Carver's secretary to come and fetch her. She was
a little surprised that getting in to see the man in the hal-
lowed halls of his own office had been so easy. For a few
misguided seconds she nurtured the improbable fantasy
that perhaps Damien Carver wasn't quite the monster Phillipa had made him out to be.

The fantasy didn't last long. No one ever got to the

stratospheric heights of success that this man obviously had by being kind, forgiving and compassionate.

What was she doing here? What was she hoping to achieve? Her sister had stolen information, had been well and truly suckered by a man who had used her to access files he wanted, had been caught and would have to face the long arm of the law.

Violet wasn't entirely sure what exactly the long arm of the law in this instance would be. She was an art teacher. Espionage, theft and nicking information couldn't have been further removed from her world. Surely her sister couldn't have been right when she had wailed that there was the threat of prison?

Violet didn't know what she would do if her sister wasn't around. There were just the two of them. At twenty-six, she was four years older than her sister and, whilst she would have been the first to admit that Phillipa hadn't always been an easy ride, ever since their parents had died in a car crash seven years previously, she loved her to bits and would do anything for her.

She looked around her and tried to stem the mounting tide of panic she felt at all the acres of marble and chrome surrounding her. She felt it was unfair that a simple glass building could fail to announce such terrifyingly opulent surroundings. Why hadn't Phillipa mentioned a word of this when she had first joined the company ten months ago? She pushed aside the insidious temptation to wish herself back at the tiny house she had eventually bought for them to share with the proceeds left to them after their parents' death. She valiantly fought a gut-wrenching instinct to run away and bury herself in all the school preparations she had to do before the new term began.

What on earth was she going to say to Mr Carver?

Could she offer to pay back whatever had been stolen? To make some kind of financial restitution?

Absorbed in scenarios which ranged from awkward to downright terrifying, she was startled when a tall grey-haired woman announced that she had come to usher her to Damien Carver's office.

Violet clutched her bag in front of her like a talisman and dutifully followed.

Everywhere she turned, she was glaringly reminded that this was no ordinary building, despite what it had cruelly promised from the outside.

The paintings on the walls were dramatic abstract splashes that looked mega-expensive…the plants dotting the foyer were all bigger and more lush than normal, as though they had been routinely fed on growth hormones… the frowning, determined people scurrying from lift to door and door to lift were younger and more snappily dressed than they had a right to be…and even the lift, as she stepped into it, was abnormally large. She dodged the repeated reflection of her nervous face and tried to concentrate on the polite conversation being made.

If this was his personal secretary, then it was clear that she had no idea of Phillipa's misdeeds. On the bright side, at least her sister's face hadn't been reprinted on posters for target practice.

She only surfaced when they were standing in front of an imposing oak door, alongside which two vertical sheets of smoked glass protected Damien Carver from the casual stares of anyone who might be waiting in his secretary's outside office.

Idly tabulating the string of idiotic mistakes Phillipa Drew had made in her half-baked attempt to defraud his company, Damien didn't bother to look up when his door was pushed open and Martha announced his unexpected visitor.

'Sit!' He kept his eyes glued to his computer screen. Every detail of his body language suggested the contempt of a man whose mind had already been made up.

With her nerves unravelling at a pace, Violet slunk into the leather chair directly in front of him. She wished she could direct her eyes to some other, less forbidding part of the gigantic room, but she was driven to stare at the man in front of her.

'He's a pig,' Phillipa had said, when Violet had off-handedly asked her what Damien Carver was like. Violet had immediately pictured someone short, fat, aggressive and unpleasant. Someone, literally, porcine in appearance.

Nothing had prepared her for the sight of one of the most beautiful men she had ever seen in her life.

Raven-black hair was swept away from a face, the lines and contours of which were finely chiselled. His unsmiling mouth filled her with cold fear but, in a strangely detached way, she was more than aware of its sensual curve. She couldn't see the details of his physique, but she saw enough to realise that he was muscular and lean. He must have some foreign blood in him, she thought, because his skin was burnished gold. He made her mouth go dry and she attempted to gather her scattered wits before he raised his eyes to look at her.

When he finally *did* turn his attention to her, she was pinned to the chair by navy-blue eyes that could have frozen water.

Damien looked at her for a long time in perfect silence before saying, in a voice that matched his glacial eyes, 'And who the hell are you?'

Certainly not the woman he had been expecting. Phillipa Drew was tall, slim, blonde and wore the air of some of the women he had dated in the past—an expression of smug awareness that she had been gifted with an abundance of pulling power.

This woman, in her unflattering thick black coat and her sensible flat black shoes, was the very antithesis of a fashion icon. Who knew what body was lurking beneath the shapeless attire? Her clothes were stridently background, as was her posture. Frankly, she looked as though she would have given a million dollars to have been anywhere but sitting in his office in front of him.

'I'm Miss Drew... I thought you knew...' Violet stammered, cringing back because, without even having to lean closer, she was still overwhelmed by the force of his personality. She was sitting ramrod-erect and still clutching her handbag to her chest.

'I'm in no mood for games. Believe me, I've had one hell of a fortnight and the last thing I could do with is someone finding their way into my office under false pretences.'

'I'm not here under false pretences, Mr Carver. I'm Violet Drew, Phillipa's sister.' She did her best to inject some natural authority into her voice. She was a teacher. She was accustomed to telling ten- and eleven-year-olds what to do. She could shout *Sit!* as good as the next person. But, for some reason, probably because she was on uncertain ground, all sense of authority appeared to have abandoned her.

'Now why am I finding that hard to believe?' Damien vaulted upright and Violet was treated to the full impact of his tall, athletic body, carelessly graceful as he walked around her in ever diminishing circles. Very much like a predator surveying a curiosity that had landed in his range of vision. He withdrew to perch on the edge of his desk, obliging her to look up at him from a disadvantageous sitting position.

'We don't look much alike,' Violet admitted truthfully. 'I've grown up with people saying the same thing. She inherited the height, the figure and the looks. From my mother's side of the family. I'm much more like my dad was.' The rambling apology was well rehearsed and spoken on autopilot; God knew she had trotted it out often enough, but her mind was almost entirely occupied with the man in front of her.

On closer examination, Damien could see the similarities between them. He guessed that their shade of hair colour would have been the same but for the fact that Phillipa had obviously dyed hers a brighter, whiter blonde and they both had the same bright blue eyes fringed with unusually dark, thick eyelashes.

'So you've come here because...?'

Violet took a deep breath. She had worked out in her head what she intended to say. She hadn't banked on finding herself utterly distracted by someone so sinfully good-looking and the upshot was that her thoughts were all over the place.

'I suppose she sent you on a begging mission on her behalf, did she?' Damien interjected into the lengthening silence. His lip curled. 'Having discovered that her sobbing and pleading and wringing of hands didn't cut it, and having tried and failed to seduce me into leniency, she thought she'd get you to do her dirty work for her...'

Violet's eyes widened with shock. 'She tried *to seduce you*?'

'A short-sighted move on her part.' Damien swung round so that he was back in front of his computer. 'She must have mistaken me for the sort of first-class idiot who could be swayed by a pretty face.'

'I don't believe it…' And yet, didn't she? Phillipa had always had a tendency to use her looks to get her own way. She had always found it easy to manipulate people into doing what she wanted by allowing them into the charmed space around her. Boys had always been putty in her hands, coming and going in a relentless stream, picked up and discarded without a great deal of thought for their feelings. Except, with Craig Edwards, the shoe had been on the other foot and life had ill prepared her to deal with the reversal. Violet was horribly embarrassed on her sister's behalf.

'Believe it.'

'I don't know if she told you, but she was used by a guy she had been dating. He wanted to get access to whatever files he thought you had on…well, I'm not too sure of the technical details…'

'I'll help you out there, shall I?' Damien listed the range of information that had fortunately never found its way into the wrong hands. He sat back, folded his hands behind his head and looked at her coldly. 'Shall I give you a rough idea of how much money my company stood to lose had your sister's theft proved successful?'

'But it *didn't*. Doesn't that count for *something*?'

'What argument are you intending to use to try and save your sister?' Damien drawled without an ounce of compassion. 'The *got-sadly-caught-up-with-the-wrong-guy* one or the *but-it-didn't-work* one? Because I can tell you now that I'm not buying either. She told me all about the smooth-talking banker with an eye to the main chance and a plan to take a shortcut to a career in computer software by nicking my ideas, except your sister, from the brief acquaintance I had with her, didn't exactly strike me as one of life's passive victims. Frankly, I put her down as a co-conspirator who just didn't have the brains to pull it off.'

Violet looked at him with loathing. Underneath the head-turning good looks, he was as cold as a block of ice.

'Phillipa didn't ask me to come,' she persisted. 'I came because I could see how devastated she was, how much she regretted what she had done...'

'Tough. From where I'm sitting, it's all about crime and punishment.'

Violet paled. 'She's being punished already, Mr Carver. Can't you see that? She's been sacked from the first real job she's ever held down...'

'She's twenty-two years old. I know because I've memorised her personnel file. So if this is the first real job she's ever held down, then do you care to tell me what she's been doing for the past...let's see...*six years*...? Ever since she left school at sixteen? If I'm not mistaken, she led my people to believe that a vigorous training course in computers was followed by exemplary service at an IT company in Leeds... A glowing written and verbal reference was provided by one *Mr Phillips*...'

Violet swallowed painfully as a veritable expanse of quicksand opened up at her feet. What could she say to that? Lie? She refused to. She looked at the hatefully confident expression on his face, the look of someone who had neatly led the enemy into a carefully contrived trap. Phillipa had said nothing to her about how she had managed to secure such a highly paid job at a top-rated company. She knew how now. Andrew Phillips had been her sister's boyfriend. She had strung him along with promises of love and marriage as he had taken up his position at an IT company in Leeds. He hadn't been out of the door for two seconds before she had turned her attention briefly to Greg Lambert and then, fatally, to Craig Edwards.

'Well?' Damien prompted. 'I'm all ears.' A part of him was all too aware that he was being a little unfair. So this girl, clearly lacking in guile, clearly well intentioned, had plucked up the courage to approach him on her sister's behalf. Not only was he in the process of shooting her down in flames, but he was also spearheading the arrow with poison for added measure.

The past few weeks of stress, uncertainty and unwelcome self-doubt were seeking a target for their expression and he had conveniently found one.

'Look—' he sighed impatiently and leaned forward '—it's laudable of you to come here and ten out of ten for trying, but you clearly need to wake up to your sister's true worth. She's a con artist.'

'I know Phillipa can be manipulative, Mr Carver, but she's all I have and I can't let her be written off because she's made a mistake.' Tears were gathering at the back of her eyes and thickening her voice.

'My guess is that your sister's made a number of mistakes in her life. She's just always been able to talk her way out of them by flashing a smile and baring her breasts...'

'That's a horrible thing to say.'

Damien gave an elegant little shrug of his shoulders and continued to look at her in a way that made her whole body feel as though it was burning up. 'I find that the truth is something best faced squarely.' Except, he privately conceded, that was something of a half truth. He had nonchalantly refused to face the truth about his mother's concerns over his lifestyle, preferring to stick it all on the back burner and turn a blind eye.

'So what happens now?' Violet slumped, defeated, in the chair. It had been a vain hope that she could appeal to his better nature.

'I'll take advice from my lawyers but this is a serious charge and, as such, has to be dealt with decisively.'

'When you say *decisively*...' She was mesmerised by

the icy, unforgiving lines of his face. It was like staring at someone from another planet. Her friends were all laid-back and easy-going. They cared about humanitarian issues. They joined protest marches and could argue for hours over the state of the world. The majority of them did charity work. She, herself, visited an old people's home once a week where she taught basic art. She had only ever mixed with people who thought like her. Damien Carver not only didn't think like her, she could tell that he was vaguely contemptuous of what she stood for. Those merciless eyes held no sympathy for anything she was saying. She could have been having a conversation with a block of marble.

'Jail.' Why beat about the bush? 'A learning curve for your sister and an example just in case anyone else thinks they can get away with trying to rip me off.'

'Phillipa wouldn't last a day in a prison cell...'

'Something she should have considered before she decided to try and hack into my computers to get hold of sensitive information,' Damien responded drily.

'It's her first offence, Mr Carver... She's not a criminal... I understand that you won't be giving her any references...'

Damien burst out laughing. Was this woman for real? 'Not *giving her references*? Have you heard a single word I've just said to you? Your sister will be put into the hands of the law and she will go to prison. I'm sure it won't be a hardcore unit with serial killers and rapists but that's not my problem. You can go visit her every week and she can productively use the time to reflect on the wisdom of a few personality changes. When she's released in due course back into the big, wide world, she can find herself a menial job somewhere. I'm sure the process of rehabilitation will be an invaluable experience for her. Of course, she'll have a criminal record, but, like I said, what else could she have expected?' He reached into one of the drawers in his massive desk, fetched out a box of tissues and pushed it across to her.

Violet shuffled out of her chair and snatched the box from his desk. Her eyes were beginning to leak. What else was there to say?

'Don't you have *any* sense of compassion?' she whispered in a hoarse undertone. 'I promise I'll make sure that Phillipa doesn't put a foot astray *ever again*…'

'She won't be able to when she's behind bars. But, just out of curiosity, how would you manage to accomplish that feat anyway? Install CCTV cameras in her house? Or flat? Or wherever it is she lives? As long-term solutions go, not a practical one.'

'We share a house,' Violet said dully. She dabbed her eyes. Breaking down was not the way to deal with a man like this. She knew that. Men like him, *people* like him, only understood a language that was similar to the one they used, the harsh and ugly language of cold, merciless cruelty. He wouldn't appreciate a sobbing female and he just wouldn't get the concept of loyalty that had driven her to confront him face to face in his own office.

Unfortunately, being tough and aggressive did not come naturally to Violet. She might have possessed a strength of character her sister lacked, but she had never had the talent Phillipa had for confrontation. 'And I would never dream of spying on anyone. I would keep an eye on her…make sure she toed the line…' Easier said than done. If Phillipa decided to try and defraud another company, then how on earth would she, Violet, ever be able to prevent her? 'I've been doing that ever since our parents died years ago…'

'How old are you?' The connections in his brain were beginning to transmit different messages now. He stared at her carefully. Her eyes were pink and her full mouth was still threatening to wobble. She was the picture perfect portrait of a despairing woman.

'Twenty-six.'

'So you're a scant four years older than your sister and I guess you were forced to grow up quickly if you were left in the role of caretaker... I'm thinking she must have been a handful...' For the first time in weeks, that feeling of being oddly at sea, at the whim of tides and currents over which he had no control, was beginning to evaporate.

Wrong-footed by the sudden change of tempo in the conversation, Violet met those fabulous navy eyes with a puzzled expression. She wondered whether this was a prelude to another rousing sermon on the salutary lessons to be learnt from incarceration. Maybe he was about to come out with another revelation, maybe he was going to inform her in that cold voice of his that Phillipa had done more than just make a pass at him. She was already cringing in mortification at what was to come.

'She went off the rails a bit.' Violet rushed into speech because, as long as she was talking, he wasn't saying stuff she didn't want to hear. 'It was understandable. We were a close family and she was at an impressionable age...'

'And you weren't?'

'I've always been stronger than Phillipa.' He was still staring at her with that speculative, unreadable expression that made her feel horribly uneasy. 'Phillipa was the spoiled one. I got that. She was a beautiful baby and she grew into a beautiful child and then a really stunning teenager. I was sensible and hard working and practical...'

'You must be hot in your coat. Why don't you remove it?'

'I beg your pardon?'

'The central heating here is in perfect working condition. You must be sweltering.'

'Why would I take my coat off, Mr Carver? When I'm going to be leaving in a short while? I mean, I've said everything there is to say and I've tried to appeal to your better nature, but you haven't got a better nature. So there's no point in my being here, is there? It doesn't really matter what I say, you're just going to tell me that Phillipa needs to be punished, that she's going to go to prison and that she'll come out a reformed person.'

'Maybe there's another discussion to be had on the subject…'

Violet hardly dared get her hopes up. She looked at him in disbelief. 'What other discussion, Mr Carver? You've just spent the past forty-five minutes telling me that she's to be held up as an example to your other employees and punished accordingly…'

'Take the coat off.'

Violet hesitated. Eventually she stood up, awkwardly aware of his eyes on her. She harked back to what he had said about her sister trying to seduce him. She had heard the contempt in his voice when he had said that. She wondered what his thoughts would be when he saw *her* without the protective covering of her capacious coat, and then she sternly reminded herself that what she looked like was irrelevant. She had come to plead her sister's case and she would take whatever sliver of compassion he might find in his heart to distribute.

Damien watched the unflattering coat reveal a baggy long-sleeved dress that was equally unflattering. Over it was a loose-fitting cardigan that reached down to below her waist.

'So the question is this…with your sister facing a prison sentence, what would you be prepared to do for her?'

He let that question hang in the air between them. Her eyes, he absently thought as she stared at him in bewilderment, weren't quite the same shade of blue as her sister's. They were more of a violet hue, which seemed appropriate given her name.

'I would do anything,' Violet told him simply. 'Phillipa may have her faults but she's learnt from this. Not just in the matter of trying to do something she shouldn't, but she's had her eyes opened about the sort of men she can trust and the ones she can't. In fact, I've never seen her so devastated. She's practically locked herself away...'

Damien thought that a few days of self-imposed seclusion before rejoining the party scene was a laughable price to pay for a criminal offence. If that was Violet Drew's definition of her sister's *devastation* then her powers of judgement were certainly open to debate.

'So you would do anything...' he drawled, standing to move to the window, briefly looking out at the miserable grey, muted colours of a winter still reluctant to release its grip. He turned around, strolled to his desk where he once again perched on the side. 'That's good to hear because, if that's really the case, then I would say that there's definitely room to negotiate...'

CHAPTER TWO

'Negotiate? How?' Violet was at a loss. Would he ask her for some sort of financial compensation for the time his people had spent tracking Phillipa down? If no money had actually been lost, then she could hardly be held accountable for any debt incurred and, even if money had actually been lost, then there was no way that she could ever begin to repay it. Just thinking of all the money his company nearly did lose was enough to make her feel giddy.

This was not a situation that Damien liked. As solutions went, it left a lot to be desired, but where were his choices? He needed to prove to his mother that she could have faith in him, that he could be relied upon, whatever the circumstances. He needed to reassure her. If his mother wasn't stressing, then the chances of her responding well to treatment would be much greater. Who didn't know that stress could prove the tipping point between recovery and collapse in a case such as this? Eleanor Carver wanted him settled or she would fret over the consequences and that was a worst case scenario waiting to happen. He loved his mother and, after years of ships-in-the-night relationships, it was imperative that he now stepped up to the plate and presented her with a picture of stability.

The grim reality, however, was that he had no female friends. The women in his life were the women he dated and the women he dated were unsuitable for the task at hand.

'My mother has recently been diagnosed with cancer…'

'I'm so sorry to hear that…'

'Stomach cancer. She's in London at the moment for tests. As you may know, with cancer, its outcome can never be predicted.'

'No. But…may I ask what that has to do with me?'

'I have a proposal for you. One that may be beneficial to both of us.'

'A proposal? What kind of proposal?'

Damien looked steadily at the woman in front of him. On almost every level, he knew this was, at best, questionable. On the other hand, looking at the bigger picture, didn't the value of the ends more than make up for the means? Sometimes you had to travel down an unexpected road to get to the desired destination.

And now a virtual stranger, a woman he would not have looked at twice under normal circumstances, was about to be ushered into his rarefied world to do him a favour and he was well aware that she would be unable to refuse because her own protective instincts for her sister had penned her into a place in which she was helpless.

'For some time, my mother has had certain…misgivings about my lifestyle…' He realised that he had never actually verbalised any of this to anyone before. He wasn't into the touchy-feely business of sharing confidences. It was reassuring to know that Violet Drew didn't actually count as someone with whom the sharing of confidences was of any significance. He wasn't involved with her. It wasn't as though she would attach herself to anything he said and use it as a way of insinuating herself into a relationship. And yet…he still had to fight a certain hesitancy.

He impatiently swept aside his natural instinct for complete privacy. Hell, it wasn't as though he was in a confessional about to admit to an unforgivable mortal sin!

'Has she?'

'If you're wondering where this is going, then you'll have to hear me out. One thing I'm going to say, though, is that nothing I tell you leaves this room. Got it?'

'What are you going to say?'

'My mother is old-fashioned…traditional. I'm thirty-two years old and, as far as she is concerned, should be in a committed, serious relationship. With a…ah…let's just say a certain type of woman. Frankly, the sort of woman I wouldn't normally look at twice.'

'What sort of women do you look at?' Violet asked, because his remark seemed to beg further elaboration. Looking at him, the answer was self-explanatory.

'Let's just say that I tend to spend my time in the company of beautiful women. They're not the sort of women my mother has ever found suitable.'

'I still don't know what this has to do with me, Mr Carver.'

'Then I'll spell it out. My mother might not have long to live. She wants to see me with someone she thinks is the right sort of woman. Currently, I know no one who fits the bill…'

Enlightenment came in a blinding rush. 'And you think that *I* might be suitable for the role?' Violet shook her head disbelievingly. How on earth would anyone ever buy that she and this man were in any way involved? Romantically? He was aggressively, sinfully beautiful while she…

But of course, she thought, that was the point, wasn't it? Whilst his type would be models with legs up to their armpits and big, long hair, his mother obviously had a different sort of girl in mind for him. Someone more normal. Probably not even someone like *her* but maybe he figured that he didn't have time on his side to hunt down someone more suited to play the part and so he had settled for her. Because he could.

Damien calmly watched as she absorbed what he was saying. 'You're nothing like anyone I've ever dated in my life before, ergo you'll do.'

'I'm sorry, Mr Carver.' Violet wondered how such physical beauty could conceal such cold detachment. She looked at him and couldn't tear her eyes away and yet he chilled her to the bone. 'For starters, I would never lie to anyone. And secondly, if your mother knows you at all, then she'll see right through any charade you have in mind to…to…pull the wool over her eyes.'

'Here's the thing, though, Miss Drew…your sister is facing a prison sentence. Is that what you really want? Do you honestly want to condemn her to the full horrors of a stint courtesy of Her Majesty?'

'That's awful! You can't *blackmail* me…'

'Whoever said anything about blackmail? I'm giving you an option and it's an extremely generous one. In return for a few days of minor inconvenience, you have my word that I'll call the dogs off. Your sister will be able to have her learning curve without having to suffer the full force of the law, which you and I both know is what she richly deserves.' He stood up and strolled towards the impressive window, looking out for a few seconds before returning to face her. 'I wouldn't want you to think for a minute that I won't do my utmost to make sure your sister is punished should you decide to play the moral card. I will.'

'This is crazy,' Violet whispered. But she had a mental snapshot of beautiful Phillipa behind bars. She didn't possess the inner strength to ever survive something like that. She was a woman who was reliant on her beauty to get through life and that had left her vulnerable. Maybe she did indeed need to have a forceful learning curve, but prison? Not only would it destroy her, but if she ever found out that she, Violet, had rejected an opportunity to save her, then would their relationship survive? There was no large extended family on whom to rely, no one to whom either of them could turn for advice. A few second and third cousins up north…and then just old friends of their parents, most of whom they no longer saw.

'No one does stuff like this.' She made a final plea. 'Surely your mother would rather you go out with the sort of women you like rather than pretend to be with someone you don't.'

'It's not quite as simple as that.' Damien raked his fingers through his hair, suddenly restless as the need for yet more confidences was reluctantly dragged from him. 'Of course, if it were a simple case of my mother not approving of my choice of woman, then it would be regrettable, but something we could both live with.'

'But…?'

'But I have a brother. Dominic is six years older than me and he lives at home with my mother in Devon.' Damien hesitated. Nine years ago, before time and experience had done its work, he had been stupid enough to fall for a woman—so stupid that he had proposed to her. It had been an eight-week whirlwind romance that had largely taken place in bed. But she had been intelligent, a career woman, someone with whom he could envisage himself enjoying intellectual conversations. And then she had met Dominic and he had known within seconds that he had made a fatal error of judgement. Annalise had tried to cover her discomfort, and he had briefly and optimistically given her the benefit of the doubt until she had haltingly told him that she wasn't sure that she was ready to commit. He had got the message loud and clear. She could commit to him, but she would not commit to him if he came with the baggage of a disabled sibling, someone he would have to look after when his mother was no longer around. Since then, he had made sure that he kept his relationships with women short and sweet. He had never taken any of them to Devon and only a few had ever met his mother, mostly when he had had no choice.

He had to fight back his natural instinct to keep this slice of his life extremely private. It was a place to which no one was invited. However, these were circumstances he could never have foreseen and, like it or not, he would have to give the woman in front of him some background detail. It wasn't a great position in which to find himself. He restively began to prowl the room while Violet distractedly watched him. There were so many things to process that her brain seemed to have temporarily shut down and, instead, her senses were making up for the shortcoming, had heightened so that she was uncomfortably and keenly aware of the flex of every muscle in his body as he moved with economic grace around her, forcing her to twist in the chair to keep her eyes on him.

'My brother was born with brain damage,' he told her bluntly. 'He's not completely helpless, but he's certainly incapable of leading a normal life in the outside world. He is wheelchair-bound and, whilst he has flashes of true brilliance, he is mentally damaged. My mother says that he was briefly starved of oxygen when he was born. The bottom line is that he is dependent on my mother, despite the fact that he has all the carers money can buy. She believes that he needs the familiarity of a strong family link.'

'I understand. If you're not settled or at least involved with someone your mother approves of…she feels that you won't be able to handle your brother if something happens to her…'

'In a nutshell.'

Looking at him, Violet had no idea how he felt about his brother. Certainly he cared enough to subject himself to a role play he would not enjoy. It pointed to a complexity that was not betrayed by anything on his face, which remained cool, hard, considering.

'It's never right to lie to people,' Violet said and the forbidding lines of his face relaxed into a cynical smile.

'You don't really expect me to believe you, do you? When you spring from the same gene pool as your sister?'

'There must be some other way I can…make amends for what Phillipa's done…'

'We both know that you're going to cave in to what I want because you have no choice. Ironically, your position is very much like my own. We're both going to engage in a pretence neither of us wants for the sake of other people.'

'But when your mother discovers the truth…'

'I will explain to her that we didn't work out. It happens. Before then, however, she will have ample opportunity to reassure herself that I am more than capable of taking on the responsibilities that lie with me.'

Violet's head was swimming. She shakily got to her feet, but then sank back down into the chair. He was right, wasn't he. She *was* going to cave in because she had no choice. They both knew it and she hated the way he had deprived her of at least having the opportunity to come to terms with it for herself.

'But it would never work,' she protested. 'We don't even like each other…'

'Liking me isn't part of the arrangement.' Damien circled her then leant forward to rest both hands on either side of the chair and Violet squirmed back, suffocating in a wave of intense physical awareness of him. Everything about him was so overpowering. There was just *so much* of him. She found it impossible to relax. It was as if she had been plugged into an electrical socket and her normally placid temperament had been galvanised into a state of unbearable, strangulating tension.

'But your mother will see that straight away…she'll *know* that this is just a farce…'

'She'll see what she wants to see because people always do.' He needed her to. He knew he had not been a perfect son. His mother had never complained about the amount of time he spent away. She had always been fully understanding about the way work consumed his life, leaving very little room for much else, certainly very little room for cultivating any relationship of any substance, not that he had ever been inclined to have one. Her unprotesting acceptance had made him lazy. He could see that now but then hindsight was a wonderful thing.

He pushed himself away and glanced at his watch. 'I intend to visit my mother later this evening.' This time when he looked at Violet, it was assessingly. 'I'm taking it that you will agree to what I've suggested…'

'Do I have a choice?' she said bitterly.

'We all have choices. In this instance, neither of us are perhaps making the ones we would want to, but…' he gave an eloquent shrug '…life doesn't always play out the way we'd like it to.'

'Why don't you just hire an actress to play the part?' Violet glared resentfully at him from under her lashes.

'No time. Furthermore, hiring someone would open me up to the complication of them thinking that there might be more on offer than a simple business proposition. They might be tempted to linger after their job's been done. With you, the boundaries are crystal-clear. I'm saving your sister's skin and you owe me. The fact that you don't like me is an added bonus. At least it ensures that you won't become a nuisance.'

'A *nuisance*, Mr Carver?'

'Damien. However gullible my mother might be, calling me *Mr Carver* would give the game away.'

'How can you be so…so…cold-hearted?'

Damien flushed darkly. As far as he was concerned, he was dealing with a situation as efficiently as he could. Drain it of all emotion and nothing was clouded, there were no blurry lines or grey areas. His mother was ill… she was anxious about him…desperate for him to produce someone by his side whom she could see as an anchor… His task was to come up with a way of putting her mind at rest. It was the way he tackled all problems that presented themselves to him. Calmly, coolly and decisively. It was an approach that had always served him well and he wasn't going to change now.

He pushed the ugly tangle of confusion and vulnerability away. He had always felt that he was the one on whom his mother and Dominic needed to rely. After his father's death, he had risen to the challenge of responsibilities far beyond any a boy in his twenties might have faced. He had jettisoned all plans to take a little time out and had instead sacrificed the dream of kicking back so that he could immerse himself in taking over the reins of his father's company. His only mistake had been to fall for a woman who hadn't been able to cope with the complete picture and, in the aftermath, he had wasted time and energy in the fruitless pastime of self-recrimination and self-doubt. He had moved on from that place a long time ago but negative feelings had never again been allowed to cloud his thinking. Indecision was not something that was ever given space and it wasn't about to get any now.

'How I choose to deal with this situation is my concern

and my concern only. Your role isn't to offer your opinion; it's to be by my side in two days' time when I go and visit my mother. And you asked me what I meant by *a nuisance*...' There was no chance that she would become a liability. They were two people who could not have been on more opposing ends of the scale. If she hadn't told him that she didn't like him, then he would have surmised that for himself. It was there in the simmering resentment lurking behind her purple-blue eyes and in her body language as she huddled in the chair in front of him as if one false move might propel her further into his radius. Of course it didn't help that she considered herself there under duress, but even when she had first walked into his office she had failed to demonstrate any of those little signals that heralded interest. No coy looks...no encouraging half smiles...no fluttering eyelashes...

He wasn't accustomed to a reaction like this from a woman and, in any other situation, he might have been amused, but not now. Too much was at stake. So, whatever he thought, he would make his position doubly clear.

'A nuisance would be you imagining that the charade was real...getting ideas...'

Violet's mouth fell open and she went bright red. Not only had he blackmailed her into doing something she knew was wrong, but he was actually suggesting, in that *smug, arrogant* way, that she might start...*what, exactly*...? Thinking that he was seriously interested in her? Or imagining that she was interested in *him*?

He really was, a little voice whispered in her head, quite beautiful but she would never be interested in a man like him. Everything about him, aside from those staggering good looks, repelled her. Her soft mouth tightened and she looked back at him with an equal measure of coolness.

'That wouldn't happen in a million years,' she told him.

'The only reason I'm even consenting to this is because I don't have a choice, whatever you say. And how do I know that you'll keep your side of the deal? How do I know that you won't take proceedings against my sister after I've done what you want…?'

Damien leaned forward. Every line of his body threatened her. 'How do I know that you won't turn around and tell my mother what's actually going on? How do I know that you'll deliver what I need you to? I guess you could say that we're going to be harnessed to one another for a short while and we're just going to have to trust that neither of us decides to try and break free of the constraints… Now, we need to discuss the details…' He strode towards his jacket, which had been tossed over the back of the leather sofa against the wall. 'It's lunchtime. We're going to go and grab something and start filling in the blanks.'

He expected her to follow. Was he like that with *all* women? Why on earth did they put up with it? She had to half run to keep up with him, past the grey-haired secretary who looked at them both with keen interest as she was ordered to cancel all his afternoon appointments, and then back down to the foyer where, it now seemed like a million years ago, she had sat in a state of nervous panic waiting to be shown to his office.

She couldn't fail to notice the way everyone acknowledged his presence as he strode ahead of her. Conversations halted, backs were straightened, small groups dispersed. There was absolutely no doubt that he ran the show and she wondered how her sister could ever have thought that she could get away with trying to steal information from him. Perhaps she had never personally met him, but surely Phillipa would have realised, even if only through hearsay, that the man was one hundred per cent hard line? But then Phillipa had been busy losing her head to a guy who had spotted a way in to making a quick buck via a back door. Her sister, for once, had found herself being the victim of manipulation. Chances were she hadn't been thinking at all.

Her coat was back on because she had expected them to be walking to wherever he was taking her for lunch, but in fact they headed down to a lift that carried them straight to an enormous basement car park and she followed him to a gleaming black Aston Martin which he beeped open with his key.

'Tell me the sort of food you like to eat,' he said without looking at her.

'Is that the first step to pretending we know one another?'

'You're going to have to change your attitude.' Damien was entirely focused on the traffic as he emerged from the underground car park into the busy street outside. 'Two people in a relationship try to avoid sniping and sarcasm. What sort of restaurants do you go to?'

He slid his eyes across to her and Violet felt a quiver of something sharp and unidentifiable, something that slithered through her like quicksilver, making her skin burn and prickling it with a strange sensation of *awareness*.

This was a business deal. They were sitting here in this flash car, awkwardly joined together in a scheme in which neither wanted to participate but both were forced to, and she could do without her nervous system going into semi-permanent free fall.

She needed to hang on to her composure, however much she disliked the man and however much she scorned his ethics.

'I don't,' she told him evenly. 'At least not often. Sometimes after work on a Friday night. I'm an art teacher. I haven't got enough money to eat out in fancy restaurants.'

She wanted to burst out laughing because not only did they dislike each other, but they were from opposite sides of the spectrum. He was rich and powerful, she was... almost constantly counting her pennies or else saving and the only power she had was over her kids.

Damien didn't say anything. He had never gone out with a teacher. He leaned towards models, who moaned about not being paid enough...but usually it meant for the purchase of top end sports cars or cottages in the Cotswolds rather than fancy meals out. Most of them wouldn't have been caught dead in cheap clothes or cheap restaurants. They earned big bucks for strutting their stuff on catwalks. In their heads, there was always a photographer lurking round the corner so getting snapped looking anything but gorgeous and being anywhere but cool was unacceptable.

'When you say *fancy*...' he encouraged.

'What do *you* call fancy?' she asked him, because why should she be the one under the spotlight all the time?

He named a handful of Michelin-starred restaurants which she had heard of and she laughed with genuine amusement. 'I've read about those places. I don't think I'd make it to any of them, even for a special occasion.'

'Really,' Damien murmured. He altered the direction of his car.

'Really. Your mother will be very curious to discover what we see in one another. How would we have met in the first place?' For a few seconds she forgot how much she disliked him and focused on the incongruity of the two of them ever hitting it off. 'I mean, did you just see me emerging from the school where I work and decide that you wanted to come over for a chat?'

'Stranger things have been known to happen.'

But not much, Violet thought. 'Where are we going, anyway?'

'Heard of Le Gavroche?'

'We can't!'

'Why not? You said you've never eaten out at a fancy restaurant. Now's your big opportunity.'

'I'm not dressed for somewhere like that!'

'Too late.' He made a quick phone call and an attendant emerged from the restaurant to take the keys to his car. 'I eat here a lot,' Damien explained in an undertone. 'I have an arrangement that someone parks my car and brings it back for me if I come without my driver. You can't wear the coat for the duration of the meal. I'm sure what you're wearing is perfectly adequate.'

'No, it's not!' Violet was appalled. The surroundings weren't intimidating. Indeed, there was a charm and old-fashioned elegance about the place that was comforting. Damien was greeted like an old friend. No one stared at her. And yet Violet couldn't help but feel that she was out of her depth, that she just didn't look the part. She had dressed for what she had thought was going to be a difficult interview. The clothes she wore to work were casual, cheap and comfortable. She wasn't used to what she was now wearing—a stiff dress that had been chosen specifically because it was the comforting background colour of dark grey and because it was shapeless and therefore concealed what she fancied was a body that was plump and unfashionable.

'Are you always so self-conscious about your appearance?' was the first thing he asked as soon as they were seated at one of the tables in a quiet corner. He eyed her critically. He had never seen such an unflattering dress in his life. 'In addition to allowing your sister to walk free, you'll be pleased to hear that you'll benefit from our deal as well. I'm going to open an account for you at Harrods. I have someone there who deals with me. I'll give you her name, tell her to expect you. Choose whatever clothes you want. I would say a selection of outfits appropriate for visiting my mother while she's in hospital.' He looked at her horrified, outraged expression and raised his eyebrows. 'I'm being realistic,' he said. 'I may be able to pull off the *opposites attract* explanation for our relationship, but there's no way I can pull off a sudden attraction for someone who is completely disinterested in fashion.'

'How *dare* you? How *dare* you be so rude?'

'We haven't got time to beat around the bush, Violet. My mother won't care what you wear but she *will* smell a rat if I show up with someone who doesn't seem to care about her appearance.'

'I do care about my appearance!' Violet was calm by nature but she could feel herself on the verge of snapping.

'You have a sister who's spent her life turning heads and you've reacted by blending into the background. I don't have to have a degree in psychology to work that one out, but you're going to have to step into the limelight for a little while and you'll need the right wardrobe to pull it off.'

'I don't need this!'

'Are you going to leave?'

Violet hesitated.

'Thought not. So relax.' He pushed the menu towards her. 'You teach art at a school…where?' He sat back, inclined his head to one side and listened while she told him about her job. He was taking everything in. Every small detail. The more she talked, the more she relaxed. He listened to her anecdotes about some of her pupils. He made encouraging noises when she described her colleagues. She seemed to do a great deal of work for precious little financial reward. The picture painted was of a hard-working, diligent girl who had put the time and effort in while her pretty, flighty sister had taken the shortcuts.

Violet realised that she had been talking for what seemed like hours when their starters were placed in front of them. Having anticipated a meal comprised of pregnant pauses, hostile undertones and simmering, thinly veiled accusations and counter accusations, she could only think that he must be a very good listener. She had forgotten his offensive observation that she didn't take care of herself, that she had no sense of style, that she needed a new wardrobe to meet his requirements. She wanted to defensively point out that wearing designer clothes was no compensation for having personality. She was tempted to pour scorn on women who defined themselves according to what they wore or what jewellery they possessed. It took a lot of effort to rein back the impulses and tell herself that none of that mattered because none of this was real. They weren't embarking on a process of discovery about each other. They were skimming the surface, gleaning a few facts, just enough to pull off a charade for the sake of his mother. That being the case, she didn't need to defend herself to him, nor should she take offence at anything he said. His request that she buy herself a new wardrobe was no different from being told, on applying for a job working for an airline, that there would be a uniform involved.

'What sort of clothes would your mother expect me to show up in?' Once more in charge of her wits, Violet paid some attention to the food that had been placed in front of her. Ornate, as beautifully arranged as a piece of artwork, and yet mouth-wateringly delicious. 'I don't own many dresses. I have lots of jeans and jumpers and trousers.'

'Simple but classy might be good...'

'And how long would I be obliged to play this part?'

Damien pushed aside his plate to lean forward and look at her thoughtfully. Down to business. Although he had to admit that hearing about her school days had been entertaining. It made a change to sit in a restaurant with a woman who wasn't interested in playing footsie with him under the table or casting lingering looks designed to indicate what game would be played when the footsie was over. He wondered whether she had ever played footsie with a man, which made him speculate on what body was hidden under her charmless dress. It was impossible to tell.

'There will be a series of tests spanning a week. Maybe a bit longer until treatment can be transferred to Devon.'

'I expect your mother will be anxious to get back to her home... Can I ask who is looking after your brother at the moment?'

'We have a team of carers in place. But that's not your concern. You will be around while she is in London. As soon as she leaves for Devon, your part will be done. I will return with her and, during that time, I will eventually break the news that we are no longer a going concern. At that point, I intend to demonstrate that she has nothing to be worried about...' He looked at her flushed heart-shaped face and his eyes involuntarily wandered down to the swell of full breasts straining against the unforgiving lines of the severe dress she had chosen to wear.

Violet sensed the shift of his attention from his unemotional checklist of facts to her body. She didn't know how she was aware of that because his face was so unreadable, the depth of his deep blue eyes revealing nothing at all, and yet she just *knew* and she was appalled when her body reacted with a surge of intense excitement that shocked and bewildered her.

Unlike her sister, Violet's history with men could have been condensed to fit on the back of a postage stamp. One fairly serious relationship three years previously, which had ended amicably after a year and a half. They had started as friends and no one could accuse them of not having tried to take it a step further, but, despite the fact that, on paper at least, it made sense, it had fizzled out. Back into the friendship from whence it had sprung. They kept in touch and since then he had married and was living the fairy tale in Yorkshire. Violet was happy for him. She harboured the dream that she too would discover her fairy tale life with someone. She was certain that she would know that special someone the second he stepped into her life. In the meantime she kept her head down, went out with her friends and enjoyed the company of the guys she met in a group. She didn't expect to be thrown unwillingly into the company of a man of whom she didn't approve and feel anything for him bar dislike. Certainly not the dark, forbidden excitement that suddenly coursed through her body. It was a reaction she angrily rejected.

'You will agree that you'll be profiting immensely from your side of this deal…' More food was brought for them although his eyes never left her face. She had amazing skin. Clear and satiny-smooth and bare of make-up, aside from some remnants of lipgloss which he suspected she had applied in a hurry.

'You still haven't told me where we're supposed to have met.' Violet looked down and focused on yet more artfully arranged food on her plate, although her normally robust appetite appeared to have deserted her. She was too conscious of his eyes on her. Having given house room to the unwelcome realisation that there was something exciting about being in his presence, that that excitement swirled inside her with a dark persuasive force that she didn't want, not at all, she now found that she had to claw her way back to the level of composure she needed and wanted.

'At your school. It seems the least convoluted of solutions.'

'Why would you be in a school in Earl's Court, Mr Carver? Sorry, *Damien*...'

'I know a lot of people, Violet. Including a certain celebrity chef who is currently working on a programme of food in schools. Since I've set up a small unit to oversee the opening of three restaurants, all of which will be staffed by school leavers who have studied Home Economics or whatever it happens to be called these days, then it makes perfect sense that I might be in your building.'

'You haven't really, have you?' Violet was unwillingly impressed that he might be more than an electronics guru. 'I mean become involved in a set-up like that...'

'Why do you find that so hard to believe?' He shrugged. Did he want to tell her how satisfying he found this slice of semi charity work? Because certainly he didn't expect to see much by way of profit from the exercise. Did he want to explain that he knew what it felt like to have someone close who would never hold down a job? He was almost tempted to tell her about his long-reaching plan to source IT projects within his company for a department that would be fitted out to accommodate the disabled because he knew from experience how many of them were capable and enthusiastic but betrayed by bodies that refused to cooperate.

'Don't bother to answer that—' he brushed aside any inclination to deviate from the point '—this isn't a soul-searching exercise. Nor do we have the time to get into too much background detail. Like I said. You smile and leave the rest to me. Before you know it, you'll be on your merry way and everyone will be happy.'

CHAPTER THREE

'BUT *HOW*? *How* did you manage to do it? I know I keep going on about it, but it's just so…incredible!'

Phillipa was sitting across the kitchen table from Violet. In front of her inroads had already been made into a bottle of white wine. She had greeted the news of Damien Carver's unexpected leniency yesterday with stunned disbelief, incredulity, anger that Violet might be stringing her along and, finally, she had taken it on board, although Violet could tell that her vague explanations hadn't quite passed muster.

'I begged and pleaded,' Violet said for the umpteenth time. 'When did you start drinking? It's only five-thirty!'

'*You'd* be drinking too if you were in my position,' Phillipa said sulkily, unwinding her long legs, which had been tucked under her, and standing up to stretch in a lazy, languorous movement like a cat. Stress had not affected Phillipa the way it would other people. She still managed to look amazing. Although it wasn't hot inside the house because the thermostat was rigidly controlled to save money, she was wearing a thin silky vest and a matching pair of silky culottes. Violet assumed that they had been one of the many presents she had received from Craig as he had manoeuvred to get her on board with his plan.

From what Violet had gathered, he had disassociated

himself from Phillipa and denied all knowledge of what she had done. Nevertheless, he was, she had been told only an hour before by her clearly gleeful sister, who had recovered well from her devastation, out of a job and planning on leaving the country. He hadn't deleted her fast enough from his Facebook account to prevent her from maliciously charting his progress but he had as soon as she had posted a message informing the world that he was a crook and a bastard and that if anyone bought that phoney crap about better opportunities abroad then they were idiots.

'I don't suppose you managed to persuade him to let them give me a reference, did you?' Phillipa asked hopefully and Violet stifled a groan of pure despair. 'Okay, okay, okay. I get the picture. But…thanks, sis…'

'You don't have to keep thanking me every two seconds.'

'I know I can be a nightmare.' She hesitated, thought about pouring herself another glass of wine and instead reached for a bottle of water from the case on the ground next to her. 'But I've really had time to think about… everything…and I've been in touch with Andy… So I may have used him just a teeny bit in getting me that job, but he's a good guy…'

A good guy who hadn't been thinking with the right part of his body when he fudged you a dodgy reference, Violet thought.

'And he's been given the sack,' Phillipa continued glumly.

'Was he very angry with you?' She shook her head, reluctantly amused at the half smile tugging the corners of her sister's mouth.

'He adores me.'

'Even after the whole Craig Edwards fiasco?'

'I explained that I just hadn't been thinking straight at

the time... Well, we all make mistakes, don't we? Anyway, seeing that we're both out of a job...we've decided to pool our resources...'

'And do what, Pip?'

'Don't be cross, but he has a good friend out in Ibiza and we're going to take our chances there. Bar work. Some DJing...loads of opportunities... I hocked all that stuff that creep gave me; well, why should I return any of it? When he nearly got me behind bars?'

Violet sat down heavily and looked at her sister. Like a married couple, they had been hitched together for better or for worse ever since their parents had died. She was twenty-six years old and had never known what it might be like to live on her own, without having to accommodate anyone else, without having to compromise, without having to tailor her needs around her sister's. Phillipa had always done her thing and Violet had picked up whatever pieces had needed picking up. She had been the shoulder to cry on, the stern voice of discipline, the nagging quasi parent, the worried other half.

'When would you go?'

'I'm heading up to Leeds in the morning and then we'll take it from there. Andy's got to sort out the lease on his flat...get his act together... You don't mind, do you?'

'I think it's a brilliant idea.' Already her mind was leaping ahead to the following afternoon, when she would be meeting Damien's mother in hospital for the first time. She realised that she had been holding a deep breath, worrying about the possibility of Phillipa asking questions, demanding to know where she was going... Stuck at home, still smarting from losing her job under ignominious circumstances, Phillipa was bored and restless...a lethal combination given the fact that she, Violet, would be trying hard to keep a secret. If Violet was clued up to her sister's foibles, then her sister was no less talented at spotting hers, and an inability to keep a secret was high on the list of her weaknesses. Now, at least, there would be one less thing to stress about.

And perhaps this was a rut… Wasn't there always a point in time when apron strings needed to be cut?

She thought of Damien's casually dismissive remarks about her relationship with her sister and gritted her teeth to block out the mental images of him that seemed to proliferate at speed and without warning. She couldn't think of anyone else, ever, who had managed to infiltrate her head the way he had. From the minute they had parted company, half her waking time had been occupied with thoughts of him and it infuriated her that not all of them were as virulently negative as she would have liked. She harked back to the cold, arrogant words leaving his mouth and then she recalled what a sexy mouth it was…she thought of that hard slashing gesture he had made with his hand when he had condemned Phillipa to jail and then, in a heartbeat, she couldn't help but recall what strong forearms he had and how the dark hair had curled around the dull silver matt of his watch…

Enthused by a positive response, Phillipa was off. Ibiza would be great! She was sick of the English weather anyway! The club scene was brilliant! She'd always wanted to work in one! Or in a bar! Or anywhere, it would seem, where computers were not much in evidence.

She left early the following morning, with promises that she would be in touch and saying she would have to return anyway to pack some things, although she could just always buy out there because they wouldn't need much more than some T-shirts and shorts and bikinis…

Deprived of her sister's ceaseless chatter, which had veered from the high of realising that she wasn't going to be prosecuted to the bitterness of acknowledging that she'd been thoroughly used by someone she had thought to be really interested in her, Violet was reduced to worrying about her forthcoming meeting with Damien.

He had informed her, via text, that he would meet her in the hospital foyer.

'Visiting hours start at five,' he had texted. *'Meet me at ten to and don't be a second late.'*

If the brevity of the text was designed to remind her of her indebtedness to him and to escalate the level of her already shredded nerves, then it worked. By the time she was ready to leave for the hospital, she was a wreck. She had spent far too long choosing what to wear. Damien's offer of a complete new wardrobe from Harrods to replace the one he obviously thought was dull, boring and inadequate, had been rejected out of hand and she was left with only casual clothes, one of her three dresses having already been used up on her interview with him. Having sneakily checked him out on the Internet, she had had a chance to see first-hand the sort of women he went for. Tall, leggy beauties. The captions informed her that they were all models. She actually recognised a couple of them from magazines. Was it any real surprise that he had suggested funding a new wardrobe for her? His mother would have to seriously be into the concept of opposites attracting if there was any chance that they would be able to pull off the charade he had signed her up for. She was short, with anything but a stick-like figure, long, unruly hair that resisted all attempts to be tamed and, as she had quickly discovered after five seconds in his presence, was never destined to be the sort of subservient yes girl he favoured.

She wore jeans. Jeans, a cream jumper and her furry boots, which were comfortable.

He was waiting for her in the designated place at the

hospital. Violet spotted him immediately. He had his back to her and was perusing the limited supply of magazines in the small gift shop near the entrance.

For a few seconds, she had the oddest sensation of paralysis. She could barely take a step forward. Her heart began to beat faster and harder, her mouth went dry and she could feel the prickly tingle of perspiration break out over her body. She wondered how she could have forgotten just how tall he was, just how broad his shoulders were. He had removed his trench coat and held it hooked by a finger over one shoulder. His other hand was in his trouser pocket. Even in the environment of a hospital, where people were too ensconced in their own private worlds of anxiety and worry to notice anything or anyone around them, he was still managing to garner interested stares.

He turned around and Violet was pinned to the spot as he narrowed his eyes on her hovering figure. She was still wearing the shapeless, voluminous coat she had worn when she had come to the office to see him on her begging mission, but now her fair hair was loose and it spilled over her shoulders in waves of gold and vanilla. Against the black coat, it was a dramatic contrast. He doubted she ever went to the hairdresser for anything more than a basic cut, and yet he knew that there were women who would have given an arm and a leg to achieve the vibrant, casually tousled effect she effortlessly had.

'You're on time,' he said, striding towards her, and Violet instinctively fell back. 'My mother is looking forward to meeting you. I see you didn't take advantage of the offer of a shopping spree.'

'I think that either someone will like me or not like me, but hopefully it won't be because of what I happen to be wearing.' She fell into step beside him. Although she tried her best to maintain a healthy distance, there was a magnetism about him that seemed to want to draw her closer, a powerful pull on her senses that defied reason. She had to resist the strangest urge to look across at him and to just keep looking.

He was explaining that his mother had wanted to find out everything about her, that he had been sketchy on detail but had fabricated nothing at all. She had been intrigued to find out that he was dating a teacher, he said.

'And did we meet in the canteen at school?' Violet asked politely as she walked briskly to keep up with him.

'I thought I'd leave it to you to come good with the romantic touches,' Damien told her drily.

'Doesn't it upset you at all that you're lying to your own mother?'

'It would upset me more to think that her health might be compromised because she was worried about my stability.' He glanced down at her fair head. She barely reached his shoulder. He could feel her reluctance pouring through every fibre of her being and he marvelled that she could be so morally outraged at a simple deception that was being done in the best possible faith and yet forgiving of her sister, who had committed a far greater fraud. He wondered whether that was the outcome of family dynamics. Just as quickly as his curiosity reared its head, he dismissed it. He wasn't in the habit of delving too deeply into female motivations. He enjoyed women and was happy to move on before simple enjoyment could become too fraught with complications. And yet this wasn't just another female to be enjoyed, was she? In fact, enjoyment didn't actually feature on his list when it came to Violet Drew.

They had taken the lift up to the floor on which Eleanor Carver had a private room. It was a large teaching hospital with a confusing number of lifts, all of which seemed to have different, exclusive destinations to specialised departments.

'I don't know anything about *you*,' Violet said in a sudden rush of panic. She tugged him to a stop before they could enter the room where his mother was awaiting her arrival. 'I mean, I know about your brother…but where did you grow up? Where did you go to school? What are your friends like? Do you even *have* any friends?'

She had pulled him to the side, where they were huddled by the wall as the business of the hospital rushed around them.

'Now that's just the sort of thing that's guaranteed to make my mother suspicious,' Damien murmured, looking down at her into those remarkable violet eyes. 'A girlfriend who thinks that her guy is such a loser that he can't possibly have any friends. You're supposed to be crazy about me…' He reached out and trailed his finger along her cheek and for a few heart-stopping seconds Violet froze. She literally found that she couldn't breathe. The noise and clatter around her faded into a dull background blur. She was held captive by deep blue eyes that bored into her and set up a series of involuntary reactions that terrified and thrilled her at the same time. She could still feel the blazing path his finger had forged against her skin and belatedly she pulled away and glared at him.

'What are you doing?'

'I know. Crazy, isn't it? Actually touching the woman who is supposed to be head over heels in love with me. You didn't think the charade would just involve you sitting across the bed from me and making small talk for half an hour, did you?'

'I… I…'

'The occasional gesture of affection might be necessary. It'll certainly make up for the fact that we're practically strangers.' Damien pushed himself away from the wall against which he had been indolently leaning. He thought of Annalise, the wife who never was. He had fully deluded himself into thinking that he had known her. In fact, it turned out that he hadn't known her at all. He had seen the perfect picture which had been presented to him and he had taken it at face value. He had committed himself to the highly intelligent, beautiful career woman and had failed to probe deeper to the shallow upwardly mobile social climber. So the fact that he and his so-called girlfriend were strangers hardly made the union less believable as far as he was concerned.

Violet hadn't banked on gestures of affection. In fact, she had naively assumed that she *would* just be sitting across a hospital bed from him and making small talk with his mother.

'There's no need to look so uncomfortable,' he drawled lazily.

'I'm not uncomfortable,' Violet hurriedly asserted. 'I just hadn't thought about that side of things.'

'There *is* no that side of things. There's the pretence of affection.'

'Oh yes. I forgot. You only like women who are decked out in designer gear and have the bodies of giraffes!'

Damien threw back his head and laughed and a few heads turned to stare for a couple of seconds. 'Are you offended because you're not my type?' He thought of Phillipa. How on earth could two sisters be so completely different? One brash and narcissistic, the other hesitant and self-conscious? Yet, curiously, so much more genuine? Intriguing.

Violet blushed furiously. 'I think we've already established that *you're* not *my* type either!' she bristled. 'And shall we just go in now?'

'Is your moment of panic over?'

'I really dislike you, do you know that?'

'You bristle like a furious little bull terrier…'

'Thank you very much for that!'

'And entering the room with that angry expression isn't going to work…'

Violet's mouth was parted as she prepared to respond appropriately to that smug little smile on his face. His mouth covered hers with an erotic gentleness that took her breath away. He delicately prised a way past her startled speechlessness and his tongue against hers was an invasion that slammed into her with the force of a hurricane. It was the most sensational kiss she had ever experienced and all she wanted to do was pull him closer so that she could continue it. Her skin burned and she felt a pool of honeyed dampness spread between her legs. She wanted the ground to open up and swallow her treacherous body whole as he gently eased himself away to push open the door to his mother's room.

He was smiling broadly as he entered and she could not have looked more like a woman in love. He had kissed her at the right time and the right place and her flushed cheeks and uneven breathing and dilated pupils were telling a story that had no foundation in fact.

He wanted his mother to believe that they were all loved up and Violet smarted from the realisation that one clever kiss had done the job. Eleanor Carver was smiling at them both, her arms outstretched in a warm gesture of welcome.

She was smaller than Violet had imagined. Whilst her son was well over six feet tall, Eleanor Carver was diminutive in stature. She looked impossibly frail against the bed sheets but her eyes were razor sharp as she rushed into inquisitive chatter.

'Don't excite yourself, Mother. You know what the consultant said.'

'He didn't say anything about not exciting myself! Besides, how can I fail to be excited when you've brought me this delightful girl of yours to meet?'

Violet stood back and watched as Damien fussed around his mother. He was so big and so powerful and yet there was a gentleness about him as he bent down to kiss her on the cheek and make sure that she was propped up just right against the pillows. It was as though he had slowed his pace to accommodate her and it brought an unwelcome lump to Violet's throat.

'He's like a mother hen now that I'm cooped up here.' Eleanor smiled and patted him on the hand.

Violet smiled back and thought that he was more fox in the coop than innocent hen and, as if he could read her mind, Damien grinned at her with raised eyebrows.

'Violet would be the first to agree that I'm the soul of sensitivity...' He moved so that he was standing next to her and she tried not to stiffen in alarm as he slipped his arm around her.

'I'm not *entirely* sure that's the description that springs to mind...' Violet unbuttoned her coat and slipped it off. In the process, she managed to edge skilfully past him to the chair next to the bed.

Still grinning as he imagined some of the descriptions she might have had in mind for him, he wasn't prepared for the hourglass figure that took his breath away for a few shocking seconds. This was not what he had expected. He had expected frumpy, slightly overweight...someone who could perhaps do with shedding a few pounds. Was it because his expectations had been so wildly at variance with the voluptuous curves on offer now that he felt the sudden thrust of painful response? Or had his diet of thin, leggy models left him vulnerable to the sort of curvy, full-breasted figure that had once haunted his testosterone-fuelled teenage dreams?

Out of the corner of his eye, he caught his mother watching him and he stopped staring to move and stand behind Violet so that he could rest both his hands on her shoulders.

From this position, he felt no guilt in appreciating the bounty of her generous breasts. She was small in stature and a positive innocent compared to the hardened, worldly, sophisticated women he dated. She didn't have a clue how to play the games that eventually led to the bedroom. He thought that if she *did* know them, then she would refuse to play them. So the lush sexiness of her body was all the more of a turn-on. Standing behind her, he could barely drag his eyes away from her gorgeous figure.

It wasn't going to do. This wasn't about attraction or sex. This was an arrangement and he didn't need it to be complicated because his testosterone levels had decided to act up.

He pulled over the other spare chair and sat next to her because staring down at her was proving to be too much of an unwelcome distraction.

His mother had launched into fond reminiscing about his childhood. Halting her in mid-stream would have been as impossible as trying to climb Everest in flip flops, so he allowed her to chatter away for as long as she wanted. He hadn't seen her so animated since she had been diagnosed and, besides, as long as she was chatting, she wasn't asking too many detailed questions. Eventually he looked at his watch and gave a little cough to indicate departure time. He would have to admit that Violet had done well. She had certainly shown keen interest in every anecdote his mother had told and had been suitably encouraging in her remarks, whilst managing to keep them brief. Watching her out of the corner of his eye, he could appreciate what he had failed to previously when he had been too busy putting his plan into action and laying down the rules and boundary lines. She was a naturally warm, empathetic person. It was what had driven her to come and see him in defence of her sister when she must have been scared witless. It was what made her smile with genuine warmth at his mother as she triumphantly reached the punchline of her story involving him, two friends and a bag of frogs.

'We really should be going, Mother. You mustn't over tire yourself.'

'Life will be very limited for me if I can't get excited and I can't get too tired, darling. Besides, there are so many questions I want to ask you both…'

Violet sneaked a surreptitious glance at Damien's hard, chiselled profile and the memory of that kiss snaked through her, bringing vibrant colour to her cheeks. Of course he hadn't been *turned on*. As he had made abundantly clear on more than one occasion, he dated supermodels. She had been chosen to play a part because she was at his mercy and because she *wasn't* a supermodel. He had kissed her like that in order to achieve something and it had worked.

It filled her with shame that *she* had been turned on. She cringed in horror at the realisation that she had wanted the kiss to go on…and on…and on… She wondered where her pride had gone when she could be held to ransom by a man she loathed to do something of which she heartily disapproved and yet, with a single touch, find her willpower reduced to rubble.

'Damien's barely told me anything about how you two met… He said that it was a couple of months ago…but that he didn't want to say anything for fear of jeopardising the relationship…'

'Did he?' Violet glanced across, eyebrows raised. 'I didn't realise that you felt so…vulnerable…' Her voice was sugary-sweet.

Damien rested his hand over hers and idly stroked her thumb, which sent her pulses racing all over again, but, with his mother's eyes on them, what could she do but to carry on smiling?

'It's a lovable trait, isn't it? Darling?' he murmured, looking her straight in the eyes and reaching to cup the nape of her neck with his hand, where he proceeded to sift his fingers through her hair.

'So how did you meet?' Eleanor asked with avid curiosity.

'Darling—' Damien continued to caress her until every part of her body was tingling in hateful response '—why don't you tell my mother all about our…romantic first meeting…?'

'It really wasn't that romantic.' Violet tried to shift away from the attentions of his hand, which was something of a mistake as he promptly decided to switch focus from her hair to her thigh. 'Actually, when I first met your son, I thought he was rude, arrogant and overbearing…'

Damien responded by squeezing her thigh gently with his big hand in subtle warning.

'He…er…came to the school for a…er…meeting with our head of Home Economics…' The pressure on her thigh was ever more insistent but, instead of turning her off, it was having the opposite effect. How on earth could her body be so wilful? When had that ever happened? She felt faint with a dark, forbidden excitement that went against every grain of common sense and reason. She wanted to squeeze her thighs tightly shut to stifle her liquid response but was scared that if she did he would duly take note and know exactly what was going on with her rebellious body. He was, after all, nothing like the guys she knew. He was a man of the world and, even on short acquaintance, she suspected that he was as knowledgeable and intimate with the workings of the female mind as it was possible for any man to be. The thought of him second-guessing that she found him sexually attractive was mortifying.

'Do you remember how bossy you were with poor Miss Taylor?' she asked, scoring points wherever she could find them and trying hard to ignore what his hand was doing to her. Out of sight of his mother's eyes because of the positioning of the chairs, his roaming hand came to rest on her thigh just below the apex where her legs met. When she thought of how that hand would feel just there, were it against bare skin, were he able to brush the downy hair with his fingers, her brain went into instant meltdown.

'We all got the impression that you were terribly important—too important to be time wasting at a school because the CEO couldn't make it... I'll admit, Mrs Carver, that my first impressions of your son were that he was a tad on the arrogant, conceited, bossy side...thoroughly unbearable, if you want the truth...'

'And yet you couldn't tear your eyes away from me,' Damien murmured in quick retaliation. He smiled and leaned across to feather a kiss on the corner of her mouth, making sure to keep his hand just where it was. 'Don't think I didn't notice when you thought I wasn't looking...'

'Ditto,' Violet muttered in feeble response because what else could she do, short of launching into a scathing attack on everything she had decided was awful about him?

'So true.' Damien allowed himself the luxury of looking at her with lazy, speculative eyes. 'And how could I ever have guessed that underneath your shapeless clothes was the figure of a sex goddess…?'

Violet went bright red. Was he joking? Continuing with their subtle duel of words which carried an undertone that his mother would not have clocked? Was he *laughing at her*? What else? she wondered, hot and flustered under the scrutiny of his deep blue eyes. She kept her gaze pointedly averted, looking at his mother with a smile that was beginning to make her jaws ache, but every inch of her was tuned in to Damien's attention, which was focused all on her. One hundred per cent of it. She could feel it as powerfully as if a branding iron had been held to her bare skin.

'Hardly a sex goddess… There's no need to tell lies…' she mumbled with an embarrassed laugh, while trying to play half of the loving couple by awkwardly leaning towards him and at the same time taking the opportunity to snap her legs firmly shut on a hand that was getting a little too inquisitive for her liking.

'You're just what my son needs, Violet,' Eleanor confided with satisfaction. 'All those girls he's spent years going out with… I expect you have a potted history of Damien's past…?'

'Mother, please. There's no need to go down that road. Violet is very much in the loop when it comes to knowing exactly the sort of women I've dated in the past…aren't you, darling…?'

'And I find it as strange as you do, Mrs Carver, that someone as intelligent as your son could have been attracted to girls with nothing between their ears. Because that's what you've said, haven't you, dearest? I'm sure they were very pretty but I've never understood how you could ever have found it a challenge to go out with a mannequin…?'

Damien smiled slowly and appreciatively at her. Touché,

he thought. She had been gauche and awkward when she had come to him with her begging bowl on her desperate mission to save her sister's skin but he was realising that this was not the woman she was at all. Warm and empathetic, yes—that much was evident from the way she interacted with his mother. She had also been prepared for him to walk all over her if she thought it would help her sister's cause. However, freed from the constraints of having to yield to him in the presence of his mother, her true colours were emerging. She was quick-tongued, intelligent and not above taking pot shots at him under cover of a smiling façade and the occasional glance that tried to pass itself off as loving.

He found that he liked that. It made a change from vacuous supermodels. Certainly, a charade he had been quietly dreading now at least offered the prospect of not being as bad as he had originally imagined and, ever creative when it came to dealing with the unexpected, he had no misgivings about making the most of a bad deal. So she thought that she'd get a little of her own back by having fun with double entendres and thinly cloaked pointed remarks? Well, two could play at that game and it would certainly add a little spice to the proceedings.

'You're so right, my dear...' Eleanor's shrewd eyes swung between the pair of them. Their body language... their interaction...her son was set in his ways...so where did Violet Drew fit in...? How had the inveterate womaniser become domesticated by the delightful schoolteacher who seemed willing to trade punches...? And where were the airheads who simpered around him and clung like leeches? Sudden changes in appetite were always a cause for concern, as her consultant had unhelpfully pointed out. So what was behind her son's sudden change in appetite? For the first time Eleanor Carver was distracted from her anxiety about her cancer. She enjoyed crosswords and sudoku. She would certainly enjoy unravelling this little enigma.

'Of course…' she glanced down at the wedding ring she still wore on her finger and thoughtfully twisted it '…there *was* Annalise…but I expect you know all about her…?' She yawned delicately and offered them an apologetic exhausted smile. 'Perhaps you could come back tomorrow? My dear…it's been such a pleasure meeting you.' She warmly patted Violet's outstretched hand. 'I very much look forward to getting to know you much, much better… I want to find out every little thing about the wonderful girl my son has fallen in love with.'

CHAPTER FOUR

So who was Annalise?

Violet was pleased that she had not been tempted to ask the second they had left his mother's room. She didn't know, didn't care and was only going to be in his company for a short while longer in any case.

Infuriatingly, however, the name bounced around in her head over the next week and a half, as their visits to the hospital settled into a routine. They met at a predetermined time in the same place, exchanged a few meaningless pleasantries on the way up in the lift and then played a game for the next hour and a half. It was a game she found a lot less strenuous than she had feared. Eleanor Carver made conversation very easy. Little by little, Violet pieced together the life of a girl who had grown up in Devon, daughter of minor aristocratic parents. Childhood had been horses and acres of land as a back garden. There had been no boarding school as her parents had doted on their only child and refused to send her away and so she had remained in Devon until, at the age of seventeen and on the threshold of university, she had met, fallen head over heels in love with and married Damien's father, an impossibly dashing half Italian immigrant who had wandered down from London with very little to offer except ambition, excitement and love. Eleanor had decided in seconds that all three were a better bet than a degree in History. She had battled through her parents' alarm, refused to cave in and moved out of the family mansion to set up house in a little cottage not a million miles away. In due course, her parents had come round. Rodrigo Carver might not have been their first choice but he had quickly grown on them. He offered business advice on the family estate when fortunes started turning sour and his advice had come good. He had a street smart head for investment and passed on tips to Matthew Carrington that saw profits swell. In return, Matthew Carrington took a punt on his rough-diamond son-in-law and loaned him a sum of money to start up a haulage business. From that point, there had been no turning back and the half Italian immigrant had eventually become as close to his parents-in-law as their own daughter.

Violet thought that Eleanor Carver probably believed in fairy tale endings because of her own personal experience. Whirlwind romance with someone from a different place and a different background…a battle against the odds… Was that why she had accepted her son's sudden love affair with a woman who could have been from a different planet?

She had posed that question to Damien only the day before and he had shrugged and said that he had never considered it but it made sense; then he had swiftly punctured that brief bubble of unexpected pleasure by adding that it was probably mingled with intense relief that she had been introduced to a woman who wouldn't run screaming in horror at the thought of wellies, mud and the great outdoors.

For once, Violet arrived at the hospital shop ahead of schedule and was glancing through the rack of magazines when she heard him say behind her shoulder, 'I didn't get the impression that you were all that interested in the life-styles of the rich and famous...'

She spun round, heart beating fast, and in that split second, realised that the hostility and resentment she had had for him had turned into something else somewhere along the line. She wasn't sure what, but the sudden flare of excitement brought a tinge of high colour to her cheeks. When had she started *looking forward* to these hospital visits? What had been the thin dividing line between not caring what she wore because why did it matter anyway, and taking time out to choose something with him in mind? She had always felt the sparrow next to her sister's radiant plumage. She couldn't compete and so she had never tried. She had chosen baggy over tight and but-toned up over revealing because to be caught up in trying to dress to impress was superficial and counter-productive. So when had that changed?

Everything they said in that room and every fleeting show of affection was purely engineered for the sake of his mother and yet she found that she could recall each time he had touched her. She no longer started when his hand slid to the back of her neck. A couple of days ago he had casually tucked some of her hair behind her ear and she had caught herself staring at him, mouth half open, transfixed by a rush of violent confusing awareness, as if they had suddenly been locked inside a bubble while the rest of the world faded away. His mother had snapped her out of the momentary spell but it was dawning on her that lines were being crossed. She just didn't know what to do about it. She would have to find out just how long the cha-rade was destined to continue. Yes, she had made a deal but that didn't mean that she could be kept in ignorance of when the deal would come to an end. Her life was on hold while she pretended to be his girlfriend. She needed to find out when she would be able to step back to reality.

'Aren't we all?' she snapped, taking a step back and bumping into someone behind her. Flustered, she muttered apologies and then looked straight into Damien's amused blue eyes. Usually he came straight to the hospital from work. Today was an exception. He wasn't in his suit but in a pair of black jeans and a thick cream jumper. She couldn't peel her eyes away from him.

'My apologies. Shall I buy the magazine for you?'

Violet discovered that she was still clutching the magazine and she wondered why because she had had no intention of getting it. 'Thank you, but there's no need. I was just about to buy it myself.'

'Please. Allow me.' He made an elaborate show of studying the cover of the magazine. 'I dated her,' he mused, but his interest stopped short of flicking through the magazine to look further.

If that passing remark was intended to bring her back down to earth, it certainly succeeded and Violet was infuriated with herself for the time she had taken choosing which pair of jeans to wear and which jumper. Ever since he had made that revealing remark about her body, and even if it had been meant for the benefit of his mother, she had chosen her snuggest jumpers to wear, the ones that did the most for a figure like hers. Now she was reminded of just the sort of body he looked at and it wasn't one like hers.

'What's her name?' Violet wondered if it was the mysterious Annalise his mother had dropped into the conversation on that first evening.

'Jessica. At the time, she was on the brink of making it to the catwalk. Seems she got there.' He paid for the magazine and handed it over to her.

'I'm not surprised. She's very beautiful.'

And once upon a time, Damien thought, she would have encompassed pretty much everything he sought in a woman. Compliant, ornamental and inevitably disposable.

He looked down at the argumentative blonde staring up at him with flushed cheeks and a defiantly cool expression and felt that familiar kick in his loins. The complication which he had been determined to sideline was proving difficult to master. He wondered whether it was because denial was not something he had ever had the need to practice when it came to the opposite sex. When he had concocted this plan, he had had no idea that he might find himself at the mercy of a wayward libido. He had looked at the earnest, pleading woman slumped despairingly in the chair in his office and had seen her as a possible solution to the problem that had been nagging away at him. Nothing about her could possibly have been construed as challenging. There had not been a single iota of doubt in his mind that she might prove to be less amenable than her exterior had suggested.

While it was hardly his fault that his initial judgement had a few holes, he still knew that the boundaries to what they were doing had to be kept in place, although it was proving more challenging than expected. Every time he touched her, with one of those passing gestures designed to mimic love and affection, he could feel a sizzle race up his arm like an electric current. Those brief lapses of self-control were unsettling. Now, as they began moving out of the hospital shop, he stopped her before they could head for the lift.

'We need to have a chat before we go up.'

'Okay.' This would be an update on how long their little game would continue. Perhaps he had had word back from the consultant on the line of treatment they intended to pursue. When she thought of this routine coming to an end, her mind went blank and she had to remind herself that it couldn't stop soon enough.

'We could go the cafeteria but I suggest somewhere away from the hospital compound. Walking distance. There's a café on the next street. I've told my mother that we might be a bit later than usual today.'

'There haven't been any setbacks, have there?' Violet asked worriedly, falling into step beside him. 'A couple of days ago your mother said that they were all pleased with how things were coming along, that it seems as though the cancer was caught in time, despite concerns that she might have left it too late…'

'No setbacks, although my mother would be thrilled if she knew that you were concerned…are you really? Because there's just the two of us here. No need for you to say anything you don't want to. No false impressions to make.'

'Of course I'm concerned!' She stopped him in his tracks with a hand on his arm. 'I may have agreed to go through this charade because my sister's future was at stake, but your mother's a wonderful woman and of course I would never fake concern!'

Damien recognised the shine of one hundred per cent pure sincerity in her eyes. For a second, something very much like guilt flared through him. He had ripped her out of her comfort zone and compelled her to do something that went against the very fabric of her moral values because it had suited him. He had thrown back the curtain and revealed a world where people used other people to get what they wanted. It wasn't a world she inhabited. He knew that because she had told him all about her friends in and out of school. Listening to her had been like lifting a chapter from an Enid Blyton book, one where good mates sat around drinking cheap boxed wine and discussing nothing more innocuous than the fate of the world and how best it could be changed.

Still, everything in life was a learning curve and being introduced to an alternate view would stand her in good stead.

'How is your sister faring in Ibiza?' he asked, an opportune reminder of why they were both here.

Violet smiled. 'Good,' she confided. 'Remember I told you about that job she wanted? The one at the tapas restaurant on the beach?' Despite the artificiality of their situation, she had found herself chatting to Damien a lot more than she had thought she might. Taking the lift down after visiting his mother, wandering out of the hospital together, he in search of a black cab, she in the direction of the underground…conversation was always so much less awkward than silence. And he was a good listener. He never interrupted and, when he did, his remarks were always intelligent and informative. He had listened to her ramble on about her colleagues at work without sneering at them or the lives they led. He had come up with some really useful advice about one of them who was having difficulties with a disorderly class. And he had cautioned her about worrying too much about Phillipa, had told her that she needed to break out of the rut she had spent years constructing and the only way to do that would be to walk away from over-involvement in what her sister was getting up to. If Phillipa felt she had no cushion on which to fall back, then she would quickly learn how to remain upright.

Had she mentioned Phillipa and the job at the bar? Damien thought. Yes. Yes, she had. Well, they saw each other every day. The periods of time spent in each other's company might have been concentrated, but they conversed. It would have been impossible to maintain steady silence when they happened to be on their own. Admittedly, she did most of the conversing. He now knew more about the day-to-day details of her life than he had ever expected to know.

'I remember.' No references needed for a bar job. Good choice.

'Well, she got it. She's only been there two days but she says the tips are amazing.'

'Let's hope she's not tempted to put her hand in the till,' Damien remarked drily but there was no rancour in his eyes as they met hers for a couple of seconds longer than strictly necessary.

'I've already given her a lecture about that,' Violet said huffily.

'And what about the partner in crime?'

'He wasn't a *partner in crime*.'

'Aside from the forging of references technicality.'

'He's working on restoring a boat with his friend.'

'He knows much about boat restoration?'

'Er...'

'Say no more, Violet. They're obviously a match made in Heaven.'

'You're so cynical!'

'Not according to my mother. She complimented me on my terrific taste in women and waxed lyrical about the joys of knowing that I'm no longer dating women with IQs smaller than their waist measurements.'

They had reached the café and he pushed open the door and stood aside as she walked past him. The brush of his body against hers made her skin burn. So his mother was pleased with her as a so-called girlfriend. She thought back to the eye-catching brunette on the magazine cover. He must find it trying to have pulled the short straw for this little arrangement. He could have been walking into a café, or into an expensive restaurant because hadn't he already told her that the women he dated wouldn't have been caught dead anywhere where they couldn't be admired, with a leggy brunette dangling on his arm. Instead of her.

He ordered them both coffee and then sat back in his chair to idly run his finger along the handle of the cup.

'Well?' Violet prompted, suddenly uncomfortable with the silence. 'I don't suppose we're here because you wanted to pass the time of day with me. It's been nearly two weeks. The new term is due to start in another ten days. Your mother seems to be doing really well. Have you brought me here to tell me that this arrangement is over?' She felt a hollow spasm in the pit of her stomach at the prospect of never seeing him again and then marvelled at how fast a habit, even a bad one, could be turned into something that left a gaping hole when there was the prospect of it being removed.

'When I told you that our little deal would be over and done with in a matter of days, I hadn't foreseen certain eventualities.'

'What eventualities?'

'The consultants agree that treatment can be continued in Devon.'

'And that's good, isn't it? I know your mother is very anxious about Dominic. She speaks to him every day on the telephone and has plenty of contact with his carers, but he's not accustomed to having her away for such a long period of time.'

'When did she tell you this?'

'She's phoned me at home a couple of times.'

'You never mentioned that to me.'

'I didn't realise that I was supposed to report back to you on a daily basis…'

'You're *supposed* to understand the limitations of what we have here. You're *supposed* to recognise that there are boundaries. Encouraging my mother to telephone you is stepping outside them.'

'I didn't *encourage* your mother to call me!'

'You gave her your mobile number.'

'She asked for it. What was I supposed to do? Refuse to give it to her?'

'My mother plans on returning to Devon tomorrow. She'll be able to attend the local hospital and I will personally make sure that she has the best in house medical team to hand that money can buy.

'That's good.' She would miss Eleanor Carver. She would miss the company of someone who was kind and witty and the first and only parent substitute she had known since her own mother had died. There had been no breathtaking revelations to the older woman or dark, secret confessions, but it had been an unexpected luxury to feel as though no one expected her to answer questions or be in charge. 'I guess you'll be going with her.'

'I will.'

'How is that going to work out for you and your work? I know you said that it's easy to work out of the office but is that really how it's going to be in practice?'

'It'll work.' He paused and looked at her carefully. 'The best laid plans, however…'

'I hate to sound pushy but would you be willing to sign something so that I know you won't go back on what you promised?'

'Don't you trust me?' he asked, amused.

'Well, you *did* put me in this position through some pretty underhand tactics…'

'Remind me how much your sister is enjoying life in sunny Ibiza…' Damien waved aside that pointed reminder of his generosity. 'Naturally, I will be more than happy to sign a piece of paper confirming that your sister won't be seeing the inside of a prison once our deal is over.'

'But I thought it was…' Violet looked at him in confusion.

'There's been an unfortunate extension.' He delivered that in the tone of voice which promised that, whatever he had to say, there would be no room for rebuttal. 'It seems that your avid attention and cosy chats with my mother on the phone have encouraged her to think that you should accompany me down to Devon.'

'What?' Violet stammered.

'I could repeat it if you like, but I can see from the expression on your face that you've heard me loud and clear. Believe me, it's not something I want either but, given the circumstances, there's very little room for manoeuvre.' Could he be treated to anyone looking more appalled than she currently was?

'Of course there's room for manoeuvre!' Violet protested shakily.

'Shall I tell her that the prospect of going to Devon horrifies you?'

'You know that's not the sort of thing I'm talking about. I…I…have loads to do before school starts…classes to prepare for…'

Damien waited patiently as she expounded on the million and one things that apparently required her urgent attention in London before raising his hand to stop her in mid-flow.

'My mother seems to think that having you around for a few days while her treatment commences would give her strength. She's aware that you start back at school in a week and a half.' She had no choice but to do exactly what he said; Damien knew that. When it came to this arrangement, she didn't have a vote. Still, he would have liked to have her on board without her kicking and screaming every inch of the way. And really, was it so horrific a prospect? Where his mother lived was beautiful. 'She's not asking you to ditch your job and sit by her bedside indefinitely.'

'I know that!'

'If I can manage my workload out of the office, then I fail to see why you can't do the same.'

'It just feels like this is…getting out of control…'

'Not following you.'

'You know what I mean, Damien,' Violet snapped irritably. 'I thought when I accepted this…this…*assignment*… that it was only going to be for a few days and it's already been almost two weeks…'

'This situation isn't open to discussion,' Damien said in a hard voice. 'You traded your freedom for your sister's. It's as simple as that.'

'And what about when I leave Devon? When do I get my freedom back?' Violet hated the way she sounded. As though she couldn't care less about his mother or her recovery. As though the last thing in the world she wanted was to help her in a time of need. And yet this wasn't what she had signed up for and the prospect of getting in ever deeper with Damien and his family felt horribly dangerous. How could she explain that? 'I'm sorry, but I have to know when I can expect my life to return to normal.'

'Your life will return to normal—' he leaned forward, his expression grim and as cold as the sea in winter '—just about the same time as mine does. I did not envisage this happening but it's happened and here's how we're going to deal with it. You're going to put in an appearance in Devon. You're going to enjoy long country walks and you're going to keep my mother's spirit fighting fit and upbeat as you chat to her about plants and flowers and all things horticultural. At the end of the week, you're going to return to London and, at that point, your presence will no longer be required. Until such time as I inform you that your participation is redundant, you remain on call.'

Violet blanched. What leg did she have to stand on? He was right. She had effectively traded her freedom for Phillipa's. While her sister was living a carefree existence in Ibiza, she was sinking ever deeper into a morass that felt like treacle around her. She couldn't move and all decision-making had been taken out of her hands.

'The more involved I get, the harder it's going to be to tell your mother…that…'

'Leave that to me.' Damien continued to look at her steadily. 'There's another reason she wants you there in Devon,' he said heavily. 'And, believe me, I'm not with her on this. But she wants you to meet my brother.' His mother had never known the reasons for his break-up with Annalise, nor had she ever remarked on the fact that, after Annalise, he had never again brought another woman down to the country estate in Devon. The very last thing he wanted was a break in this tradition, least of all when it involved a woman who was destined to disappear within days.

'That's very sweet of her, Damien, but I don't want to get any more involved with your family than I already am.'

'And do you think that *I* do?' he countered harshly. 'We both have lives waiting out there for us.' The fact that control over the situation had somehow been taken out of his hands lent an edge to his anger. When his mother had suggested bringing Violet to Devon, he had told her, gently but firmly, that that would be impossible. He cited work considerations, made a big deal of explaining how long it took to prepare for a new term—something of which he knew absolutely nothing but about which he had been more than happy to expound at length. He had been confident that no such thing would happen. His fake girlfriend would not be setting one foot beyond the hospital room.

His mother had never been known to enter into an argument with him or to advance contrary opinions when she knew how he felt about something. He had been woefully unprepared for her to dig her heels in and make a stance, ending her diatribe, which had taken him completely by surprise by asking tartly, 'Why don't you want her to come to Devon, Damien? Is there something going on that I should know about?'

Deprived of any answering argument, he had recovered quickly and warmly assured his mother that there was nothing Violet would love more than to see the estate and get to know Dominic.

'You will need a more extensive wardrobe than the one you have,' he informed her because, as far as he was concerned, there was nothing further to be said on the matter. 'You need wellies. Fleeces. Some sort of waterproof coat. I'm taking it that you don't have any of those? Thought not. In that case, you're going to go to Harrods and use the account I've already talked to you about.'

'Do you know something? I can't wait for all of this to be over! I can't wait for when I no longer have to listen to you bossing me about and reminding me that I'm in no position to argue!' Over the past few days she had been lulled into a false sense of security, of thinking that he wasn't quite as bad as she had originally thought. She had watched him interacting with his mother, had listened as he had soothed the same concerns on a daily basis without ever showing a hint of impatience. She had foolishly started feeling a weird connection with him.

'Is that how you treat everyone?' she blurted, angry with herself for harbouring idiotic illusions. 'Is that how you've treated all the women you've been out with? Is that how you treated Annalise?' It was out before she had a chance to rein it in and his eyes narrowed into chips of glacial ice.

'Was that another topic under discussion with my mother?'

'No, of course not! And it's none of my business. I just feel…frustrated that my whole world has been turned upside down…'

'Excuse me if I don't feel unduly sympathetic to your cause,' Damien inserted flatly. 'We both know what was at stake here. As for Annalise, that's a subject best left unexplored.' Without taking his eyes from her face, he signalled for the bill.

'You can't expect me to spend a week in your mother's company and not have an inkling of anything to do with your past.' She inhaled deeply and ploughed on. 'What do you expect me to say when she talks about you? It's going to be different in Devon. We'll have a great deal more time together. Your mother's already mentioned her once. She's sure to mention her again. What am I supposed to say? That we don't discuss personal details like that? What sort of relationship are we supposed to have if we never talk about anything personal?'

She stared at him with mounting frustration and the longer the silence stretched, the angrier she became. He might be the puppet-master but there were limits as to how tightly he could jerk the strings! She foresaw long, cosy conversations with his mother when her only response to any questions asked, aside from the most basic, would be a rictus smile while she frantically tried to think of a way out. She would be condemned to yet more lying just because he was too arrogant to throw her a few titbits about his past.

'I don't *care* what happened between the two of you. I just want to be able to look as though I know what your mother's on about if she brings the name up in conversation. Why are you so…so…*secretive*?'

Damien was outraged that she had the nerve to launch an attack on him. Naturally there was a part of him that fully understood the logic of what she was saying. Undiluted time spent with his mother in front of an open fire in the snug would be quite different from more or less supervised snatches of time spent next to a hospital bed during permitted visiting hours. Women talked and it was unlikely that he could be a stifling physical presence every waking minute of the day. That said, the implicit criticism ringing in her voice touched a nerve.

Bill paid, he stood up and waited until she had scrambled to her feet.

'Are you going to say anything?' She reached out and stayed him with her hand. 'Okay, so you've had loads of girlfriends. That's fine.'

'I was going to marry her,' Damien gritted.

Violet's hand dropped and she looked at him in stupefied silence. She couldn't imagine him ever getting close enough to any woman to ask for her hand in marriage. He just seemed too much of a loner. No…it was more than that. There was something watchful and remote about him that didn't sit with the notion of him being in love. And yet he had been. In love. Violet didn't know why she was so shocked and yet she was.

'What happened?' They were outside now, heading back towards the hospital. Her concerns about going to Devon had been temporarily displaced by Damien's startling revelation.

'What happened,' he drawled, stopping to look down at her, 'was that it didn't work out. I didn't share the details with my mother. I don't intend to share them with you. Any other vital pieces of information you feel you need to equip yourself with before you're thrown headlong into my mother's company?'

'What was she like?' Violet couldn't resist asking. In her head, she imagined yet another supermodel, although it was unlikely that she could be as stunning as the one on the cover of the magazine.

'A brilliant lawyer who has since become a circuit judge.'

Well, that said it all, Violet thought. It also explained a whole host of things. Such as why a highly intelligent male should choose to go out with women who weren't intellectually challenging. Why his interest in the opposite sex began and ended in bed. Why he had never allowed himself to have a committed relationship again. He had been dumped and he still carried the scars. She felt a twinge of envy for the woman who had had such power over him. Was he still in touch with her? *Did he still love her?*

'And do you bump into her? London's small.'

'Question time over, Violet. You now have enough information on the subject to run with it.' Damien's lips thinned as he thought of Annalise. Still hovering in the wings, still imagining that she was the love of his life. Did he care? Hardly. Did he bump into her? Over the years, with tedious and suspicious regularity. There she would be, at some social function for the great and the good, always making sure to seek him out so that she could check out his latest date and update him on her career. He never avoided her because it paid to be reminded of his mistake. She was a learning curve that would never be forgotten.

Violet saw the grim set of his features and drew her own, inevitable conclusions. He had been in love with a highly intelligent woman, someone well matched for him, and his marriage proposal had been rejected. For someone like Damien, it would be a rejection never forgotten. He had found his perfect woman and, when that hadn't worked out, he had stopped trying to find another.

What they had might be a business arrangement, but everything he had ever had with every woman after Annalise had been *an arrangement*. Arrangements were all he could do.

'I'll get some appropriate clothes,' Violet conceded. 'And you can text me with the travel info. But, at the end of the week, it's over for me. I can't keep deceiving your mother.'

'By the end of the week, I think you will have played your part and I will officially guarantee that your sister is off the hook.'

'I can't wait,' Violet breathed with heartfelt sincerity.

CHAPTER FIVE

THE HOUSE THAT greeted Violet the following evening was very much like something out of a fairy tale. Arrangements for Eleanor's transfer had been made at speed. Her circumstances were special, as she was the principal carer for Dominic, and Damien, with his vast financial resources, had made sure that once the decision to transfer was made, it all happened smoothly and efficiently.

In the car, Violet had alternated between bursts of conversation about nothing in particular to break the silence and long periods of sober reflection that the task she had undertaken seemed to be spinning out of control.

She was travelling with a stranger to an unknown destination, removed from everything she knew and was familiar with, and would have to spend the next few days pretending to be someone she wasn't. If she had known what this so-called arrangement would have entailed, would she have embarked on it in the first place? Regrettably, yes, but knowing that didn't stop her feeling like a sacrificial lamb as the powerful car roared down the motorway, eating up the miles and removing her further and further from her comfort zone.

While Phillipa was taking time out in Ibiza, doing very little in a tapas restaurant and no doubt enjoying the attention of all the locals as she wafted around in sarongs and summer dresses, here she was, sinking deeper and deeper into a situation that felt like quicksand, all so that her sister could carry on enjoying life without having to pay for the mistakes she had made.

'Maybe she *should* have had her stint in prison,' Violet said, apropos of nothing, and Damien shot her a sideways glance.

Locked in to doing exactly what he required of her, he could sense the strain in the rigid tension of her body. She would rather be anywhere else on earth than sitting here in this car with him. Naturally, he could understand that. More or less. After all, who wanted to be held hostage to a situation they hadn't courted, paying for a crime they hadn't committed? Yet was his company so loathsome that she literally found it impossible to make the best of a bad job? She was pressed so tightly against the passenger door that he feared she might fall out were it not for the fact that the doors were locked and she was wearing a seat belt.

There had been times over the past week and a half when some of her resentment had fallen away and she had chatted normally to him. There had also been times when, in the presence of his mother, he had touched her and his keenly attuned antenna had picked up *something*—something as fleeting as a shadow and yet as substantial as jolt of electricity. Something that had communicated itself to him, travelling down unseen pathways, announcing a response in her that she might not even have been aware of.

'You don't mean that,' he said calmly.

'Don't tell me what I mean! If it weren't for Phillipa I wouldn't be here now.'

'But you are and there's no point dwelling on what ifs. And stop acting as though you're being escorted to a torture chamber. You're not. You'll find my mother's estate a very relaxing place to spend a few days.'

'It's hardly going to be a *relaxing situation*, is it? I don't feel *relaxed* when I'm around you.' When she thought about seeing him for hours on end, having meals in his company, being submerged in his presence without any respite except when she went to bed, she got a panicky, fluttery feeling in the depths of her stomach.

Without warning, Damien swerved his powerful car off the small road. They were only a matter of half an hour away from the house and the roads had become more deserted the closer they had approached the estate.

'What are you doing?' Violet asked warily as he killed the engine and proceeded to lean back at an angle so that he was looking directly at her. In the semi-darkness of the car, with night rapidly settling in around them, she felt the breath catch painfully in her throat. Apprehension jostled with something else—something dark and scary, the same dark, scary thing that had been nibbling away at the edges of her self-control ever since he had told her about Devon.

'So you don't feel relaxed around me. Tell me why. Get it off your chest before we reach the house. Okay, you're not here of your own free will, but there's no point lamenting that and covering old ground. It is as it is. Have you never been in a position where you had to grit your teeth and get through it?'

'Of course I have!'

'Then tell me what the difference is between then and now.'

'You're scary, Damien. You're not like other people. You don't *feel*. You're so…so…*cold*…'

'Funny. Cold is not a word that any woman has ever used to describe me…'

Violet felt her heart begin to race and her mouth went dry. 'I'm not talking about…what you're like in bed with women…'

'Would you like to?'

'No!'

'Then how would you like me to try and relax you?'

Violet couldn't detect anything in his voice and yet those words, innocuous as they were, sent a shiver of awareness rippling up and down her spine. She had a vivid, graphic image of him relaxing her, touching her, making her whole body melt until she was nothing more than a rag doll. Was this the real reason why she was so apprehensive? Terrified even? At the back of her mind, was she more scared of just being alone with him than she was of playing a game and acting out a part in a place with which she was unfamiliar? Did her own responses to him, which she constantly tried to squash, frighten her more than *he* did?

It didn't seem to matter than he was cold, distant, emotionally absent. On some level, a part of her responded to him in ways that were shocking and unfamiliar.

She could feel the lazy perusal of his eyes on her and she wished she hadn't embarked on a conversation which now seemed to be unravelling.

'I'm just nervous,' she muttered in a valiant struggle to regain her self-composure. 'I'll be fine once we get there. I guess.'

'Try a little harder and you might start to convince me. You get along well with my mother. Is it Dominic?' The question had to be asked. He hadn't been in this position for a very long time. He had brought no one to Devon. He had vowed to never again put himself in the position of ever having to witness a negative reaction to his brother. However, this was an unavoidable circumstance and he felt the protective machinery of his defences seal around him like a wall of iron.

'What are you talking about?' Violet was genuinely puzzled.

'Some people feel uncomfortable around the disabled. Is that why you're so strung out?' It had taken Annalise to wake him up to that fact, to the truth that there were people who shied away from what they didn't know or understand, who felt that the disabled were to be laughed at or rigorously avoided. The ripple effect of those reactions were not contained, they always spread outwards to the people who cared. It was good to bring this up now.

'No!'

'Sure about that, Violet? Because you know me, you know my mother…the only unknown quantity in the equation is Dominic…'

'I'm *looking forward* to meeting your brother, Damien. The only person who makes me feel uncomfortable is *you*!' This was the first time she had come near to openly admitting the effect he had on her. She glared at him defensively, feeling at once angry and vulnerable at the admission and collided with eyes that were dark and impenetrable and sent her frayed pulses into overdrive.

All at once and on some deep, unspoken level, Damien could feel the sudden sexual tension in the air. Her words might say one thing but her breathlessness, the way her eyes were huge and fixed on him, the clenching and unclenching of her small fists…a different story.

He smiled, a slow, curving, triumphant smile. Whilst he had privately acknowledged the unexpected appeal she had for him, whilst he had been honest about the charge he got from a woman who was so different in every possible way to the type of women he had become used to, he had pretty much decided that a Hands Off stance was necessary in her case.

But they were going to be together in Devon and, like an expert predator, he could smell the aroma of her unwelcome but decidedly strong sexual attraction towards him. She was as skittish as a kitten and it wasn't because she was nervous about spending a week in the company of his mother. Nor was she hesitant about his brother. He had detected the sincerity in her voice when he had suggested that she might be.

He took his time looking at her before turning away with a casual shrug and turning the key in the ignition. Her presence next to him for the remainder of the very short drive felt like an aphrodisiac. Potent, heady and very much not in the plan.

The drive up to the grand house was tree-lined, through wrought-iron gates which he could never remember being closed. Having not been to the estate for longer than he liked to think, Damien was struck by the sharp pull of familiarity and by the hazy feelings he always associated with his home life—the sense of responsibility which was always there like a background refrain. Having a disabled brother had meant that any freedom had always been on lease. He had always known that, sooner or later, he would one day have to take up the mantle left behind by his parents. Had he resented that? He certainly didn't think so, although he *did* admit to a certain regret that he had failed to extend any input for so long.

Was it any wonder that his mother had been so distraught when she had been diagnosed, that she might leave behind her a family unit that was broken at the seams? He had a lot of ground to cover if he were to convince her otherwise.

'What an amazing place,' Violet murmured as the true extent of the sprawling mansion, gloriously lit against the darkness, revealed itself. 'What was it like growing up here?'

'My parents only moved in when my grandfather died, and I was a teenager. Before that, we lived in the original cottage my parents first bought together when they were married...'

'It must have seemed enormous after a cottage...'

'When you live in a house this size you get used to the space very quickly.' And he had. He had lost himself in it. He had been able to escape. He wondered whether he had been so successful at escaping that a part of him had never returned. And had his mother indulged that need for escape? Until now? When escape was no longer a luxury to be enjoyed?

Not given to introspection, Damien frowned as he pulled up in the large circular courtyard. The house was lit up like a Christmas tree in the gathering darkness and they had hardly emerged from the car with their cases when the front door was flung open and Anne, the housekeeper who had been with the family since time immemorial, was standing there, waving them inside.

Violet wondered what her role here was to be. Exactly. Sitting by a hospital bed, she had known what to do and the impersonal surroundings had relieved her of the necessity of trying to act the star-struck lover. A few passing touches, delivered by Damien rather than her—more would have seemed inappropriate in a hospital room, where they were subject to unexpected appearances from hospital staff.

But here she was floundering in a place without guidelines as they were ushered into the grandest hall she had ever seen.

The vaulted ceiling seemed as high and as impressive as the ceiling of a cathedral. The fine silk Persian rug in the hall bore the rich sheen of its age. The staircase leading up before splitting in opposite directions was dark and highly polished. It was a country house on a grand scale.

The housekeeper was chatting animatedly as they were

led from the hall through a perplexing series of rooms and corridors.

'Your mother is resting. She'll be down with Dominic for dinner. Served at seven promptly, with drinks before in the Long Room. You've been put in the Blue Room, Mr Damien. George will bring the bags up.'

Looking sideways, Violet was fascinated at Damien's indifference to his surroundings. He barely looked around him. How on earth could he have said that a person could become accustomed to a house of this size? She had initially been introduced to Anne as his girlfriend and now, as though suddenly remembering that she was trotting along obediently next to him, he slung one arm over her shoulder as the housekeeper headed away from them through one of the multitude of doors, before disappearing into some other part of the vast family mansion.

'An old retainer,' he said, dropping his arm and moving towards a side staircase that Violet had failed to notice.

'It's a beautiful house.'

'It's far too big for just my mother and Dominic, especially considering that the land is no longer farmed.' He was striding ahead of her, his mind still uncomfortably dwelling on the unexpected train of thought that had assailed him in the car, the unpleasant notion that the grand house through which he was now confidently leading the way had been his excuse to pull away from his brother. He had never given a great deal of thought to his relationship with Dominic. Was he now on some kind of weird guilt trip because of the circumstances? Had he shielded himself from the pain Annalise had inflicted on him when she had rejected his brother by pulling ever further away from Dominic? He should have been far more of a presence here on the estate, especially with his mother getting older.

'It would be a shame to sell it. I bet it's been in your

family for generations…' She was barely aware of the bedroom until the door was thrown open and the first thing that accosted her was the sight of a massive four-poster bed on which their suitcases had been neatly placed. While he strode in with assurance, moving to stand and look distractedly through the windows, she hovered uncertainly in the background.

'Well?' Damien harnessed his wandering mind and focused narrowly on her.

'Why are both our suitcases in this room?' Violet asked bluntly. She already knew the answer to that one, yet she shied away from facing it. She hadn't given much thought to the details of their stay. In a vague, generalised way, she had imagined awkward one-to-one conversations with Damien and embarrassing economising of the truth with his mother, along with stilted meals where she would be under scrutiny, forced to gaily smile her way through gritted teeth. She hadn't gone any further when it came to scenarios. She hadn't given any thought to the possibility that the loving couple might be put in the same bedroom. She had blithely assumed that such an eventuality would not occur because surely Eleanor belonged to that generation which abhorred the thought of cohabitation under their roof. Eleanor was a traditionalist, a widow who still proudly wore her wedding ring and tut tutted about the youth of today.

'Because this is where we'll be sleeping,' Damien replied with equal bluntness. His unaccountably introspective and dark frame of mind had not put him in the best of moods. Having questioned his devotion as a son and on-hand supportive presence as a brother, the last thing he needed was to witness his so-called girlfriend's evident horror at being trapped in the same bedroom as him.

'I can't sleep in the same room as you! I didn't think that this would be the format.'

'Tough. You haven't got a choice.' He began unbuttoning his shirt, a prelude to having a shower, and Violet's eyes were drawn to the sliver of brown chest being exposed inch by relentless inch. She hurriedly looked away but, even though she was staring fixedly at his face, she could still see the gradual unbuttoning of his shirt until it was completely open, at which point she cleared her throat and gazed at the door behind him.

'There must be another room I can stay in. This place is enormous.'

'Oh, there are hundreds of other rooms,' Damien asserted nonchalantly. 'However, you won't be in any of them. It's a few days and my mother has put us together. Somehow I don't think she's going to buy the line that we're keeping ourselves virtuous for the big day.' He pulled off his shirt and headed towards his case on the bed, flipping it open without looking at her. 'We have roughly an hour before we need to be downstairs for drinks. My mother enjoys the formal approach when it comes to dining. It's one of her idiosyncrasies. So do you want to have the bathroom first or shall I?'

Violet hated his tone of voice. It was one which implied that he couldn't even be bothered to take her concerns into account. He was accustomed to sharing beds with women, she thought with a burst of impotent anger. In his adult life, he had probably slept with a woman next to him a lot more often than he had slept alone. It wasn't the same for her. Did he imagine that she would be able to lie next to him and pretend that she was on her own? The bed was king-sized but the thought of moving in the night and accidentally colliding with his sleeping form was enough to make her feel like fainting.

'I hate this,' she whispered, filled with self-pity that the last vestige of her dignity was being stripped away from her. 'You'll have to sleep on the sofa.'

Damien glanced at the chaise longue by the window and wondered whether she was being serious. 'I'm six foot four. What would you suggest I do with my feet?' He raised his eyebrows and watched as she struggled in silence to come up with a suitable response. 'I've spent hours driving. I'm going to have a shower. Don't even think of trawling the house for another bedroom.'

With that, he vanished into the adjoining bathroom, leaving Violet to fight off the waves of panic as she stared at her lonesome suitcase on the bed. Everything about the bedroom seemed designed to encourage a fainting fit, from the grandeur of a bed that would have been better suited to the lovers they most certainly were not, to the thick, heavy curtains which she imagined would cut out all daylight so that the intimacy of the surroundings became palpable.

Wrapped up in a series of images, she almost forgot that he was in the shower until she heard the sound of water being switched off, at which point she raced to her suitcase, extracted an armful of clothes and then stood to attention by the window, with her back pointedly turned to the bathroom door.

She heard the click of the door opening and then she froze as his voice whispered into her ear, 'You can look. I'm decently covered. Anyone would think that you were sweet sixteen and never been kissed.'

He was laughing as she unglued her eyes from his bare feet and allowed them to travel upwards to where he was decently covered in no more than a pair of boxer shorts and his shirt, which he was taking his own sweet time to button up.

If he called that *decently covered* then she wanted to

ask him what she might expect of him when the lights were switched off.

'I'll meet you downstairs,' she said coolly, at which he laughed a bit more.

'You wouldn't have a clue where to go,' Damien pointed out. Her face was flushed. Her hair, which had started the journey in a sensible coil at the nape of her neck, was unravelling. He could feel his mood beginning to lift, which was a good thing because he was ill equipped for negative thoughts. 'You'd need a map to find your way round this house. At least until you've become used to it. Most of the rooms aren't used but good luck locating the ones that are.' He reached into the cupboard where a supply of clothes, freshly laundered, were hanging, awaiting his arrival.

Once again, Violet primly averted her eyes as he slipped a pair of trousers from a hanger. She backed towards the door but he wasn't looking at her.

Good heavens! She would have to get her act together if she was going to survive her short stay here. She couldn't succumb to panic attacks every time they were alone together! She would need immediate counselling for post-traumatic stress disorder as soon as she returned to London if she did! He wasn't even glancing in her direction. If he could be unaffected by her presence, then she would follow his lead and everything would be smooth sailing. Two adults sharing a room wasn't exactly a world-changing event, she told herself once she was in the bathroom, having checked the door three times to make sure that it was locked.

She took a long time. She had bought a couple of dresses so that she didn't have to spend the entire stay in jeans and sweaters. This dress, a navy-blue stretchy wool one with sleeves to her elbows, was fitted, although she couldn't quite see how fitted because there was no long mirror in the bathroom. Nor could she do much with her make-up because the ornate mirror over the double sink was cloudy with condensation. Her hair, she knew, was fit for nothing except leaving loose. Her curls were out of control, a tangle of falling tendrils which she impatiently swept back from her face before taking a deep breath and opening the bathroom door.

He was sprawled on the bed, the picture of the Lord of the Manor waiting for his woman to emerge. His trousers were on, although, her inquisitive eyes made out, zipped but with the button undone. His long-sleeved jumper was dark grey and slim-fitting, so there was no escaping the lean, hard lines of his body.

One arm behind his head, Damien watched her with brooding eyes. It was the first time he had ever seen her in a dress that actually fitted. More than that, it clung. To curves that did all the right things in all the right places and lovingly outlined the sort of breasts that mightn't work on a catwalk but sure as hell worked everywhere else. He forgot about any tension that might lie ahead. He forgot those vague, never disclosed concerns that he had turned a blind eye to his brother for too long. Hell, he forgot pretty much everything as his eyes raked over her body and he felt the pain of an erection leaping to attention. Which made him hurriedly sit up.

She was running her fingers through her hair and wincing as she tried to gently unravel some of the knots. Then, without saying a word, she flounced over to her case and excavated a pair of high-heeled shoes which she self-consciously slipped on with her back to him.

'I'm ready.' She smoothed nervous hands along the dress. This wasn't the sort of thing she ever wore. She had always favoured baggy. She wondered whether her stupid brain had actually paid attention to that passing compliment he had given her about her figure and then decided that if it had, she was pathetic. But she still felt a thrill of excitement as he lazily scrutinised her before shifting off the bed, taking his time and moving at an even more leisurely pace to retrieve his watch from the dressing table.

'I hope I look okay…' Violet was mortified to hear herself say and she was even more mortified when, with deliberate slowness, he eyed her up and down and then up and down again for good measure.

'You'll do. New dress?'

'You can have it back when this stint is over.'

'What would I do with it?'

'I just wouldn't want you to think that I wanted anything from you but my sister's freedom.'

'I've always found martyrdom an annoying trait.'

Violet seethed on the way down, through another wilderness of rooms. En route, he gave her a potted history of the house and the land around it. She thawed. She was reluctantly charmed at the thought of an unknown half Italian coming to live there and passing on the mansion to his children, wrenching it away from the exclusive grasp of the landed gentry.

By the time they were finally at the sitting room where drinks were being served, she was more relaxed, and then she fully relaxed as Eleanor was helped down to make her entry, accompanied by Dominic and a young girl who tactfully left, having settled Eleanor in the chair by the fire.

She forgot about Damien. She knew that she should be making conspicuous efforts to play the adoring girlfriend but she became wrapped up in Eleanor and Dominic. She had been warned about Dominic's disability. She hadn't been told that although he was in a wheelchair, although his speech was often difficult to understand and although his movements were not perfectly controlled, he was smart and he was funny and shy. She sat very close to him, sipping her wine and leaning in so that she could pick up everything he said while Damien and his mother conducted a conversation, the wisps of which came floating her way. The need to think about selling the house…the difficulties of managing the various floors even if she made a full recovery…the value of having somewhere closer to civilisation where doctors and the hospital were not an unsafe car drive away if the weather was inclement.

He was the background voice of reason, the head of the family making sensible decisions, although, sliding her eyes across to him, she was aware of the frustration etched on his features at his mother's vague, non-committal replies to his persuasive urgings.

Every family had its stories to tell and she wondered if this was his. If he was so embedded in his role as protector that he failed to recognise any form of mutiny in the ranks. He obviously didn't think that his brother should have any input because the conversation was dropped the minute they were at the dinner table.

A carer helped Dominic with his food while Eleanor fussed and explained to her that that was normally her job.

'I'm a pain in the ass,' Dominic stammered.

Violet laughed and looked across to Damien, who was seated opposite her. 'You have that in common with your brother,' she said tartly and then flushed when he looked back at her with a slow, appreciative smile. Her heartbeat quickened. His glance lingered just that bit too long and she returned it with just a little too much dragging intensity.

After that, she was conscious of every little movement he made and tuned in to every word he said, even when her attention appeared to be elsewhere. She was aware of the quality of the food and the fact that she was being treated like a valued guest because, despite what Damien had said, Eleanor had long dispensed with formalities when it was just herself and Dominic and the wonderful girl who helped with him. Then they ate in the kitchen with dishes served by the housekeeper straight from Aga to plate.

'My son would know that if he visited with a bit more regularity,' Eleanor said with asperity. 'Perhaps you could see that as your mission—to get him away from London and his never ending workload…'

Watching her, Damien was impressed at how well she fielded the awkward remark, which implied a future that wasn't on the cards. He took in the way she communicated with Dominic. With ease, not patronising, without a hint of indulgence or condescension. Nor did she look to anyone to rescue her from what she might have felt was an uncomfortable situation.

Sipping the espresso that had been brought in for him, he mentally began to compare her natural responses to those of Annalise but it was an exercise he killed before it could take root. Such comparisons, he knew, were entirely inappropriate. That said, he murmured softly as they walked back up the stairs, Dominic and his mother having retired for the night, 'Very good…'

'Sorry?' Violet wished she could have stretched the evening out for longer—for as long as she could, like a piece of elastic with no breaking point—because now she faced the prospect of the shared bedroom. He certainly wasn't going to sleep on the chaise longue. *She* could try to, but chaises longues had not been designed for deep REM slumber. She might embarrass herself by falling off. Worse, she might *hurt* herself by falling off.

'Your performance tonight. Very good.'

'I wasn't performing.' They were now at the bedroom door and she stood back as he pushed it open and waited for her to precede him. 'You know I like your mother and your brother's amazing.' He was pulling off the luxurious, ornate spread that had been thrown over the bed, dumping it in a heap in the corner of the room. Violet's hands itched to fold it neatly, a legacy of having an untidy sister behind whom she had long become accustomed to tidying up.

He was beginning to unbutton his shirt, eyes still firmly focused on her, pinning her into a state of near paralysis.

Why couldn't he have found somewhere else to sleep? Or found *her* somewhere else to sleep? Surely, in a mansion the size of a hotel, they could have had separate sleeping quarters without the whole world detecting it? Why was she being placed in this position? It felt as though every sacrifice was being made by *her* and she was the one who directly benefited from none of it.

Anger at her helplessness to alter the situation made her eyes sting. She clung to the anger like a drowning person clinging to a lifebelt.

'I can see why your mother was so worried about Dominic when she was diagnosed,' Violet imparted recklessly and she immediately regretted the outburst when he stilled.

'Come again?'

'Nothing,' Violet mumbled.

'Really?' He was strolling towards her, lean, dark and menacing, and Violet stood her ground, stubbornly defensive. 'If you have something to say, why don't you come right out and say it? Only start something, Violet, if you intend to see it through to the end.'

'Well, you don't seem to really communicate with him. You leave it all to your mother. I heard you talking about selling the house with her and yet you didn't say anything to Dominic about it, even though he would be affected as well…'

Damien stared at her with cold fury. Had he just heard

correctly? Was she actually *criticising* his behaviour? Coming hard on the heels of his own unexpected guilt trip, he could feel rage coursing through his veins like a poison. Was she deliberately needling him?

'I don't seem to communicate with him…' was all that managed to emerge from his incredulous lips.

'You talk around him and above him and when you *do* talk directly to him, you don't really seem to expect an answer, even though you look as if you do.'

'I can't believe I'm hearing this.'

'No one ever tells you like it is, Damien.'

'And you mistakenly think that you're in a position to do so?' He watched as she lowered her eyes, although her soft lips were still pinched in a stubborn line. 'This may come as a cruel shock, but you're over-stepping your brief…'

When had he stopped listening to what his brother had to say? Was it when they moved to the estate? When acres of space removed the need for physical proximity? And then later, in London…with trips back to the estate infrequent obligations…his mother usually amenable to taking a bit of time out in London, travelling without Dominic… had distance crept through the cracks until he had simply forgotten how to communicate? Or, worse, had he selfishly been protecting himself by unconsciously withdrawing? You couldn't feel pain at other people's thoughtless reactions if you just never put yourself in that position in the first place, could you?

'I know I am!' Violet flung at him defiantly. 'But you can't expect me to come here and have no opinions at all on the people I meet! And besides, what do I have to lose by telling you the truth? Once I leave here, I'll never see you again! And maybe it's time someone *did* speak their mind to you!' She had courted an argument. It seemed safer to get into that bed with her back angrily turned away from him. But the shutter that fell over his eyes sent a jolt of unhappiness through her. She fought it off because why did it matter what he thought of her in the long run?

'I think I'll go downstairs and catch up on work.' Damien turned away from her, walked towards his laptop, which he had left on the chest of drawers, and Violet was unaccountably tempted to rush into a frantic apology for having crossed the line.

'Don't,' he threw over his shoulder with biting sarcasm, 'wait up.'

CHAPTER SIX

WHEN DAMIEN HAD considered the challenge of setting his mother's fears to rest and allaying her worry that he would not be able to cope with Dominic in her absence, he had envisaged a fairly straightforward solution.

He would take time off work to come to Devon. He would dispatch Violet after her week and, henceforth, he would assume the mantle of responsible son and dependable brother. How hard could it possibly be? He might have been a little lax in his duties over the years, but that was not for lack of devotion to his family. His work, every minute of it, was testimony to his dedication. They wanted for nothing. His brother had the very best carers money could buy. His mother enjoyed help on every front, from garden to house. She fancied roses? He had ensured that a special section of the extensive cultivated land was requisitioned for a rose garden fit to be photographed in a magazine. When she had been complaining of exhaustion only months previously, before the reason behind that exhaustion became known, he had personally seen to it that one of the finest chefs in the area was commissioned to cook exquisite meals and deliver them promptly so that she could be spared the effort of doing so herself. On the rare occasions when she ventured up to London, theatre tickets had been obtained, opera seats reserved, tables at the best restaurants booked.

Unfortunately, his clear cut route now to a successful outcome was proving elusive.

He adjusted his tie, raked his fingers through his hair and then hesitated. He knew that Violet was more than happy to meet him in the sitting room. After five days, she knew that house better than he did. How had that transpired? Because she was involving herself with his family. She and his mother appeared to have become best buddies. From his makeshift office in the downstairs library, he had a clear view of the back garden and had spotted them out there in the cold, slowly strolling and chatting. About what? He had casually asked her a couple of days ago and she had shrugged and delivered a non-answer. Was he going to push it? No. Ever since she had decided that it was her right to speak her mind, she had defied all attempts to smooth the strained atmosphere between them. In company, she was compliant and smiling. The second they were alone together, he was treated to the cold shoulder despite the fact that he had magnanimously chosen to overlook her outrageous, uninvited criticism of him.

He pulled the chair over to the window and sat down. At six-thirty in the evening, the room was infused with the ambers and golds of what had been a particularly fine and sunny day. In an hour, they would be leaving for a local restaurant. This had not been of his choosing. He would have been more than happy to have had a meal in, relaxed for ten minutes and then retired to catch up on his emails. But his mother had suggested it, to take her mind off the treatment which was due to commence at the weekend.

Or maybe, he mused darkly, Violet had suggested it… who was to say? His mind idly wandered over the events of the past few days. The clever way she had bonded with

Dominic, involving him in the art preparation she was doing for her class, letting him guide her through some computer stuff for a website she wanted to set up to display the work of her more talented pupils. His mother had taken him to one side and confided that she had never seen Dominic so relaxed with anyone.

'You know how wary he is of people he doesn't know...' she had murmured.

He didn't, in actual fact. Which had only served as a reminder of what Violet had said about his communication skills.

He scowled and then looked up as the door to the adjoining bathroom slowly opened.

Immersed in her thoughts, with a towel wound turban style around her newly washed hair and another towel wrapped round her body, barely skimming her breasts and thighs, Violet was not expecting him. In fact, she didn't register him at all sitting on the chair in the far corner of the room.

She was thinking about the past few days. Having a view on Damien and his relationship with his family seemed to have been the catalyst for the one thing she had been determined to avoid, namely involvement. She had told him what she thought about his relationship with his brother and, in so doing, she had unlocked a door and stepped inside the room. She hadn't wanted to have opinions. She had simply wanted to do her time and then disappear back to her life. Instead, she was becoming attached and she had no idea where that was going to lead. Damien was barely on speaking terms with her. They communicated in front of an audience but once the audience was no longer around, the act was dropped and he disappeared into that office of his, only emerging long after she was fast asleep.

The bed which she had looked at with horror, which had thrown her into a state of panic because she had had visions of rolling over and bumping into him, had turned out to be as safe as a chastity belt. She was not aware of him entering the room at night because she was fast asleep and she was not aware of him leaving it in the morning because she was still sleeping.

She pulled the towel off her head and shook her hair, then she walked towards the bedroom door and locked it because you could never be too sure. Damien would already be downstairs. He would be making an effort.

Just like that, her mind leapt past her own nagging worries and zeroed in on Damien. She no longer fought the way he infiltrated her head. One small passing thought and suddenly the floodgates would be opened and she would lose herself in images of him. It was almost as if the connections to her brain were determined to disobey the orders given and merrily abandon themselves to reformatting her thoughts so that he played the starring role.

Without even looking in his direction, she was still keenly aware of everything he did and everything he said. There was no need to look at him because in her mind's eye she could picture the way he looked, his expressions, the way he had of tilting his head to one side so that you had the illusion that whatever you were saying was vitally important.

He had stopped trying to corner his mother into making a decision about the house and whether it should be sold.

He had begun asking her about small things, like books she might have read and committees she belonged to in the village.

His conversation with Dominic was no longer a few words, some polite murmurings, a hearty pat on the shoulder and then attention focused somewhere else. Over dinner the evening before, she had heard him telling his brother about one of his deals which had run into unexpected problems with the locals because a vital factory had been denied planning permission, and the trouble they had taken to accommodate their concern.

Violet would rather not have noticed any of these details. She would rather he remained the one-dimensional baddy who barely had two words to say to her the second they were alone. She didn't want to leave this house only to find herself wondering how the rest of their lives all turned out. She wanted to be able to put them all out of her mind and yet, the more absorbed she became in their dramas, the more difficult she knew that was going to be.

Still frowning, she dropped the towel to the floor and stepped towards the wardrobe. Her hair felt damp against her back and she lifted the heavy mass with one hand and, at that very moment, she saw him.

For a few seconds Violet thought her eyes might be playing tricks on her. She froze, her arm still raised holding her hair away from her body. Her brain refused to accommodate the realisation that he wasn't safely downstairs but was, in fact, watching her as she stood in front of him, completely and utterly naked. When it did, she gave a squeak of absolute horror and reached for the discarded towel, which she wrapped tightly around her body. She was shaking like a leaf.

'What are you doing here?' She backed towards the bathroom door but, before she could make it to the relative safety of the bathroom, he was standing in front of her, barring her path.

For the first time in his life, Damien was lost for words. What was he doing there? Did it make any difference that it was his bedroom?

The thirty-second glimpse of her body had sent his libido into orbit. He was in physical pain and he fought to bring his senses back down to Planet Earth. The fluffy white towel was back in place, secured very firmly by tightly clenched fists, but in his mind's eye he was still seeing the voluptuous curves of her body. He had caught himself idly wondering what she looked like under the dresses and the jeans and the jumpers. Whenever he had entered the bedroom to find her asleep, the covers had been pulled tightly up to her neck as though, even in slumber, she was determined to make sure that she kept him out. The first time he had seen her in jeans, his imagination had been up and running and her deliberate attempts to keep him at arm's length had only served to increase its pace.

But nothing had prepared him for the mind-blowing sexiness of her curves. Her breasts, unrestrained by a bra, were far more than a generous handful. Her nipples were big pink discs that pouted provocatively and her stomach was flat as it planed downwards to the thatch of dark blonde hair between her thighs. All thoughts of self-denial were shattered in an instant. Every ounce of common sense that warned him against getting involved with a woman whose departure date from his life was any minute now, vanished like a puff of smoke.

'You have to go,' Violet said shakily. 'I want to get dressed.' She just couldn't look him in the face. Her body was burning at the thought of his eyes on it. Even with the towel secured around her, she still felt as though her nudity was on parade.

'I wanted to talk to you.'

'We can talk…later…your mother and Dominic…'

'Will be fine if they have to wait for us for a few minutes.'

He stood in front of her, as implacable as a solid wall of granite. Having made a concerted effort in the past few days to try and give her body as little option as humanly possible to feel any of that unnerving, unwelcome sexual awareness that seemed to ambush her at every turn, she was horribly aware of her racing pulses and the liquid heat pooling inside her. The silence stretched and stretched. She desperately wanted to get dressed and yet shied away from drawing attention to her nakedness under the towel.

'I need to get dressed,' she finally breathed and Damien stood aside.

Now that he had dropped all pretence of keeping life simple by not yielding to an attraction that seemed to have a will of its own, he could feel the stirrings of a dark, pervasive excitement coursing through him. Anticipation was a powerful aphrodisiac.

'Of course,' he murmured, stepping back further. 'We can talk later.' And they would.

Violet only realised that she had been holding her breath when she sagged against the closed bathroom door. Her breathing was thick and uneven. After days of standoff, she had felt those lazy eyes on her naked body and nearly collapsed. What did he want to talk to her about? She had heard the slam of the bedroom door, but she gave it a little while before poking her head out and establishing that the bedroom was empty.

She wanted to put that recollection of him sitting in that chair, looking at her as she blithely discarded the towel, to the back of her mind. Actually, she wanted to eradicate it completely, but it kept recurring as she got dressed and met the assembled party in the Long Room.

What had he thought of her? Had the reality of a body that wasn't stick-thin repulsed him? She had returned to her uniform of baggy clothes, a shapeless dress over which she had thrown a thick cardigan. The thought of drawing any more attention to herself made her feel sick. At least there

would be more than just the four of them for the meal out.
Eleanor had invited some of her friends. Damien's attention would be blessedly diluted. But, even amidst the upbeat conversation and the laughter, she was keenly aware
of his eyes sliding over to her every so often. The conversation finally turned to Eleanor's treatment, which was
due to start the following day.

'No one can tell me exactly how I'll be affected,' she
confessed to one of her friends who had undergone a similar situation and was full of upbeat advice. 'Apparently,
everyone reacts differently…but it'll be wonderful knowing that I'll have Dominic and Damien by my side…' She
looked steadily at Damien. 'You *will* be staying on for a
short while, won't you, darling?'

Damien smiled and gave an elegant, rueful and play-
fully resigned shrug. 'My office is up and running. It'll
make a nice change looking through the window and not
being treated to a splendid London view of office blocks…'

He did it so well, Violet thought, returning to her food.
He was charm personified. Everyone was chuckling. There
was general laughter when he launched into a wry anecdote about some of the urban myths surrounding a couple
of the office blocks in the square mile.

When the laughter had died down, Eleanor turned to
Violet. 'You must hate me for keeping Damien all the way
down here in this part of the world…' she murmured.

Violet flushed. She hated those instances when she had
felt horribly as though she was doing more than just play
acting for a good reason, when she felt corralled into a corner from which she had no choice but to baldly lie.

'Oh, I shall be busy…you know…the new term starts
soon and it's always hectic…' she offered vaguely.

'But you *will* come down on the weekends, won't you,
my dear? You've been such a source of strength…'

'Well…sure, although…er…Damien mentioned something about having office stuff to do in London…in the coming weekends…'

'Did I?' Damien looked at her with a perplexed expression. 'I've been known to go to the office occasionally on a weekend, but…' he raised both hands in a gesture of amused surrender while keeping his eyes firmly pinned to Violet's flushed face '…even a diehard workaholic like myself knows when to draw the line…so I'll be down here unless something exceptional happens in London that requires my presence…'

'So that means that you'll be with us this weekend, my dear?' Eleanor was looking keenly at Violet's flushed face. 'I shall probably need some help around the house and it's so much nicer having someone around who knows us all rather than getting staff in. I do know you'll be busy at school…so please say if you'd rather not come…perfectly understandable…'

Violet felt the weight of expectation from everyone around the table and she sneaked a pleading glance at Damien, who returned her stare with an infuriatingly bland expression. 'I…' she stammered. 'I'm sure I should be able to…get away for the weekend…given the circumstances…' She smiled weakly. Even to her own ears, it was hardly the sound of excited enthusiasm but Eleanor was smiling broadly and reached over to pat her on her hand.

'Perfect! I shall probably be in a horizontal position most of the time but it should give you and Damien a really terrific opportunity to explore the village and the surroundings. I mean, you've hardly been out on your own since you got here and I may be an old lady but I'm not so old that I can't remember what it's like to be a couple of love birds…!'

Everyone laughed. Dominic said something salacious. Violet cringed.

She barely registered the remainder of the evening. She drank slightly more than was usual for her. By the time they eventually made it back to the house, it was after ten-thirty and her few glasses of wine had gone to her head.

'You need water,' Damien said, leading her towards the kitchen once Eleanor and Dominic had disappeared. 'And paracetamol...you drank too much.'

'Don't you dare lecture me on how much I drank, Damien!' She yanked her arm free of his supportive hand, stumbled, straightened and stopped to glare at him. 'How *could* you?'

Damien wondered whether she was aware that she was slurring her words. Ever so slightly. She had also, some-where along the line, hurriedly done up her cardigan but misaligned the buttons and her hair was all over the place as she had insisted on opening her car window for a spot of fresh air.

'You're going to have to sit down if you're going to ac-cuse me of something.' He led her towards a kitchen chair, sat her down and fetched her a glass of water and some tablets. 'Now...' he positioned his chair squarely to face her and leaned forward, resting his forearms on his thighs and staring at her with earnest concentration '...you were about to start an argument...'

Violet was mesmerised by his eyes. He hadn't shaved for the day and there was a dark shadow that promised stubble in the morning. She wanted to reach out and touch it. The temptation was so strong that she had to sit on her hand to suppress it.

'So tell me what I'm guilty of,' Damien prompted, 'but only when you've finished looking at me. I wouldn't want to rush that...'

Violet reddened and immediately looked away. 'So now I'm going to be coming here at the weekend,' she said in a rush. The feel of his eyes on her and the faint woody smell of his aftershave were doing disastrous things to her equilibrium, cutting a swathe straight through the cool detachment she had managed to maintain over the course of the past few days. After his reciprocal coldness, this sudden attention was as dramatic on her nerves as an open flame next to dry tinder.

'I do recall you agreeing to something of the sort.' Damien was enjoying her attention. Enjoying the way her eyes skittered away from his face but then were compulsively drawn back to stare at him. He realised how much he had disliked her coolness towards him. They might have found themselves sharing the same space for very dubious reasons, but proximity and their need to pretend had invested a certain edge to what they had. A little wine had now made her lower her defences and he liked that. A lot. He leaned a little closer, as though he didn't want to miss a single word of what she was saying.

'Are you telling me that you didn't mean it?' he asked in a vaguely startled voice, as though this angle had only now popped into his head. 'Perhaps I misconstrued the relationship you have with my mother. You two seemed to be getting along like a house on fire…'

'That doesn't have anything…to do with…anything…' Violet said incoherently. 'I *like* your mother very much. *That's* why I…why it's such *a mistake*…'

'Honestly not following you at all…'

'I was only supposed to be here until the end of the week…'

'You were. And you're free to go once your week here is over.' He sat back, angling his body to one side so that he could extend his legs. He linked his hands behind his head.

'You have a life happening back in London. Of course, I know that I could keep you hanging on, doing what I ask of you, because you would do pretty much anything to save your sister's skin, but...' He stood up and walked, loose-limbed, to fetch himself a bottle of water, which he drank in one go while he continued to stare at her.

'But?' Violet was still having trouble peeling her eyes away from him.

'But that could prove a never-ending situation. So once we're back in London, feel free to jump ship. I'll sign a guarantee that your sister won't be prosecuted. She will be free as a bird to roam the Spanish coastline doing whatever takes her fancy. And you can return to your life.'

'And what would you tell your mother?' Faced with the prospect of returning to her life, Violet was now assailed by a host of treacherous misgivings that this much-prized life, the one she had insisted was there, waiting to be lived, was not quite the glittering treasure she had fondly described. She didn't quite get it, but there had been a strange excitement to being in Damien's company. When she was around him, even when, as had been the case over the past few days, she was keeping her distance, she was still always so *aware* of him. It was as if her waking moments had been injected with some sort of life-enhancing serum.

'That's not your problem. You can leave that one to me.'

'I'd quite like to know,' Violet persisted. She should be grabbing at this lifeline. She knew that. 'I'm really fond of your mother, Damien. I wouldn't want to think...I wouldn't want her to...'

'Be unduly hurt? Become stressed out? Think badly of you? All of the above? Funny, but I wasn't getting the impression that you were overly bothered. After all, five seconds ago you were accusing me of deliberately blindsiding you by not announcing on the spot that you wouldn't be back here for weekends…'

'I thought you would *want* to start bracing your mother for…you know…the inevitable…'

'The day before she begins what could be gruelling treatment?'

'Well…'

'Dominic has become attached to you.'

'Yes…' Just something else to think about, just another link in the chain she would have to melt down when she walked away from his family.

'When my mother begins her treatment she'll probably be too weak to help with my brother…'

'He doesn't need *help* as such. I mean, he has his carers for the physical stuff…'

'But has always relied on my mother for everything else. If she's in bed, she won't be able to provide all of that.'

'Which could be where *you* step in,' Violet urged him.

Damien flushed darkly. This conversation wasn't meant to be about *him*. Her bright eyes were positively glowing with sincerity.

'I can't be on call twenty-four seven. I still have a business to run, even if it's from a distance.'

'You wouldn't have to *be on call* twenty-four seven. Dominic's perfectly happy doing his own thing. He's really got into that website I asked him to try and design… Besides, I've noticed…'

'What? What have you noticed?'

'You didn't like it the last time I spoke my mind.'

'Maybe I've realised that it's about time I stop trying to think of your mind as anything but a runaway train,' Damien mused under his breath.

'I don't think that's very fair.' All signs of tipsiness had evaporated. She felt as sober as a judge. Her hands were clammy as she rested them on her knees to strain forward.

'You speak your mind. Maybe I find that a refreshing change. So don't spoil the habit of a lifetime now by going coy on me.'

'Okay. Well, I've noticed that you're making a bigger effort with Dominic. I mean, when we got here, you were hardly on speaking terms with him.'

Considering he had asked her to speak her mind, Damien made a concerted effort to control his reaction to that observation. 'Go on,' he muttered tightly, through gritted teeth.

'You never really directly *talked* to him. You talked *at* him, then you turned your attention to someone else or something else. And yet,' she mused thoughtfully, 'your mother says you two used to be so close when you were growing up...'

So *that* was what they talked about, Damien thought tensely. They discussed *him*. He angrily swept aside the sudden undercurrent of guilt that had been his unwelcome companion over the past few days and rose to his feet.

'It's late. We should be heading up,' he said smoothly.

'*We*? Aren't you going to work?'

'I'll see you up to the bedroom first. My mother would be horrified if you missed your footing on the stairs because you had a little too much to drink and I wasn't there to do the gentlemanly thing and catch you as you fell...'

'You're annoyed with me because of what I've said...'

'You're entitled to have your opinions.'

'I never wanted to.' She rose a little clumsily to her feet and turned in the direction of the kitchen door.

'Never wanted to what...?'

His breath fanned her cheek as he leaned down to hear what she was saying.

'Have opinions. I never wanted to have opinions about you.' She felt giddy and breathless as he shadowed her out of the kitchen and into the series of corridors and halls that eventually led to the staircase up to the wing of the house in which they had been placed.

'I'm finding that so hard to believe, Violet,' he murmured in a voice that warmed every part of her. 'You *always* have opinions. When you first walked into my office, I took you for someone who had scrambled all her courage together to confront me but who, under normal circumstances, wouldn't have said boo to a goose. My mistake.'

Violet eyed the landing ahead of her. Bedroom to the right. She thought she had recovered from that momentary tipsiness induced by a little too much wine with dinner but now she felt dizzy and flustered and wondered if she had overestimated her sobriety after all.

She glanced down and her eyes flitted over his lean brown hand on the banister just behind her.

Her heart was beating wildly as they made it to the bedroom door.

'All teachers have opinions,' she managed in a strangled voice. She took a step back as he reached around her to push open the bedroom door.

'There's a difference between having opinions and being opinionated. You're opinionated.' His arm brushed her and, all at once, he felt himself harden at the passing contact. That forbidden excitement coursed through him, reminding him of what she had looked like standing in front of him, naked and unaware. He hadn't had a woman for over three months. His last relationship, short-lived though it had been, had crumbled under the combined weight of his unreliability and her need to find out where they were heading. Not even her stupendous good looks, her unwavering availability whatever the time of day or night, or the very inventive sex, could provide sufficient glue to keep them going for a little longer.

He firmly closed the door behind him and switched on a side light so that the bedroom was suddenly infused in a mellow, romantic glow.

'You're going downstairs to work now, aren't you?' Violet asked nervously and he gave her a rueful smile.

'I'm trying to kick back a little…I think it would reassure my mother that I'm capable of involving myself in family life and leaving the emails alone now and again… You do approve, don't you?'

Violet found herself in the unenviable position of having to agree with him, especially when she had stuck her head above the parapet to voice her positive opinions on just that point.

'So…if you'll excuse me, I'll go have a shower…' He began unbuttoning his shirt and was amused when she primly diverted her eyes. This was the very situation most women would have loved. Up close and personal with him in a bedroom. He caught the distinctly erotic aroma of inexperience and her shyness was doing amazing things for his already rampant libido.

He made sure not to lock the door but he took his time, washing his hair and emerging twenty minutes later to find her with all her accoutrements in her hands.

'Sure you don't need a suitcase to carry all that stuff through?' he enquired and Violet blushed.

'I wouldn't want to disturb you when I come out. Just in case you're sleeping.'

'Very thoughtful.'

Violet backed away, eyes pinned to his face, anywhere but his muscled body, which was completely naked but for the tiny towel he had slung around his waist and which was dipping down in a very precarious fashion.

Did he sleep in pyjamas? How would she know when he had spent the past few nights retiring to bed at after one in the morning and getting up before six to start his day? She certainly hadn't seen any lying about and she found that her mind was entirely focused on that one small technicality as she lingered in the bathroom for as long as she possibly could.

And for a while after she emerged into a pitch-black room, she actually breathed a sigh of relief that he was asleep. He was nothing more than a dark shadow on the bed. On the very *big* bed.

Barely daring to breathe, she slipped under the duvet and turned on her side away from him with movements that were exaggeratedly slow. *Just in case.*

'You never actually told me whether you'd decided to come next weekend or not. Our conversation must have become waylaid…'

Violet gave a squeak of horror that he was not only awake but, from the sound of his voice, bright-eyed and bushy-tailed. She heard him adjust his position on the bed and when he next spoke she knew that he was now facing her.

'I think we lost track of the point when you decided to congratulate me on my sterling efforts with my brother…' He reached out to place a cool hand on her shoulder and Violet's blood pressure soared into the stratosphere. 'I hate talking to someone's back.'

Violet froze. She felt trapped between a rock and a hard place. She was in this bed with this man and she either turned round to face him, thereby instantly diminishing the generous proportions of the bed, or else she remained as she was, with her back to him like a petrified object, desperately hoping that hand would go away and not do something more exploratory to urge her over onto her other side. She reluctantly shifted her position and was screamingly aware of the rustle of the duvet and the soft deflation of the pillow as her body shifted.

Her eyes had adjusted to the darkness in the bedroom and her mouth went dry when she realised that he was bare-chested. Propping himself up on one elbow, the duvet was down to his waist, allowing her an eyeful of his perfectly muscled, sinewy chest with its flat brown nipples and just the right amount of dark hair to make her breath catch painfully in her throat.

'That's better,' Damien said with satisfaction. 'Now I can actually see your face. So what's your decision to be?'

'Can't we discuss this in the morning?'

'I'm a great believer in not putting off for tomorrow what can be done today and that includes decisions.'

'I suppose it wouldn't hurt to come down next weekend,' Violet mumbled. Underneath the prim fleecy pyjamas, she could feel the heavy weight of her unconstrained breasts, which in turn made her remember that very moment when she had realised he had been watching her as she had emerged completely naked from the bathroom. Those twin attacks on her crumbling composure sent a wave of heat licking through her.

'My mother and Dominic will both be pleased.' Damien's voice was low and unbearably sexy. 'As,' he continued, 'will I...'

'You will? You don't mean that. You've barely spoken to me all week.'

'I might say the same for you. But we're talking now...'

'Yes...'

'Feels good, doesn't it?'

Violet could hear the rapid rush of her own breathing. His low, husky words were a backdrop to something else. She felt it with an instinct she wasn't even aware she possessed. He wasn't touching her but it felt as though he might be and, although she knew that he couldn't read her expression any more accurately than she could read his in the darkness, there was still a crackle of high voltage electricity between them that made the hairs on the back of her neck stand on end.

Was he going to make a move on her? Surely not! And yet…now was the time to briskly bring the conversation to an end by turning away. Sleep might be difficult to court with him lying right there next to her on the bed, but he would get the message that she had nothing more to say to him when she coldly turned away. And if she couldn't see him, then this weirdly unsettling *awareness* that was making her pulses race would be extinguished at source. He would probably be gone, as usual, before she woke up in the morning and they would be back to keeping a healthy distance from each other, only breaking it in front of his family.

Violet knew exactly what she should do and how she should react and instead, to her horror, she found herself reaching out to touch that hard, broad chest. Just one touch. Where on earth had that dangerous thought come from? How had it managed to slip through all the walls and barriers of common sense and self-protection she was frantically erecting?

And where had that soft gasping sound come from as her fingers rested briefly on his chest?

Damien felt a kick of supreme satisfaction. Never had a woman's touch felt so good. It was hesitant, timid, a barely-there sort of touch, and it ignited his blood, which was burning hot in his veins as he pulled her towards him…

CHAPTER SEVEN

His lips met hers and Violet was lost. While a part of her knew that this shouldn't be happening, the rest of her clung to him with shameful abandon. She couldn't get enough of touching him. She wanted to explore every inch of his body and then begin all over again. The urge was nothing like anything she had felt before in her life. For her, love-making always seemed a calm, pleasant business, but then her one and only lover had started life as a friend. Damien was certainly no friend and this was not calm. She feverishly traced the muscled contours of his shoulders and she could feel him smiling against her mouth.

She ran her foot along his calf and shivered as her knee came into contact with the rigidity of his erection. When he flipped her onto him, she arched and threw her head back as he undid the buttons of her top, to reveal breasts that dangled tantalisingly by his mouth. She straightened to fling the constricting fleece off her.

She looked down at him, breathing hard, her hair tumbling past her shoulders. His skin was golden-brown, a natural bronze that contrasted dramatically against her own paleness. She reached out and flattened the palm of her hand against him and felt the ripple of muscle under her fingers.

He pulled her into him and half groaned as her breasts

squashed against his chest. This time, his kiss was long, lingering and never-ending. It was a kiss that was designed to get lost in. It was a kiss that allowed no room for thought.

The warm fleece of her pyjama bottoms felt itchy and uncomfortable. Her underwear was damp with spreading moisture. She parted her legs and, through the fleece, she felt the hard jut of his erection.

'We shouldn't,' she moaned, instantly negating that passing thought by moving sinuously against him.

'Why? We both want it...'

'Because you want something doesn't mean that you should just go right ahead and have it...'

'Are you telling me that you want to stop?' She could no more do that than he could. Damien was aware of this with every fibre of his being. He pulled her back down against him, stifling any protest she might have come up with, and Violet ran her fingers through his hair. She loved the feel of its silky thickness. Touching him like this...it felt decadent, taboo, weirdly wicked. Even though she was supposed to be his girlfriend...

She felt like a Victorian maiden on the verge of swooning when he eased her up and hooked his fingers into the waistband of the pyjamas. Her breasts were tempting and luscious, but first...

He tugged the bottoms and watched with satisfaction as she quickly slipped them off. When she reached to do the same with her panties, he stayed her hand. He could see the dampness darkening the crotch as she straddled him and he placed his palm against the spot and moved it until he could feel the wetness seeping through to his hand.

'Enjoying yourself?' Anticipation was running through his veins. Making his blood boil. He intended to take things slowly, but it was hard. All he could think of was her settling on him, feeling her softness sheathing him and her tightness as she moved on him. 'Touch me.'

Violet quivered. The underwear had to come off. She was going crazy. She swung her legs over the side of the bed and kicked it free, then turned back to see him watching her with a little smile as he touched himself. He was huge. A massive rock-hard rod of steel nestled in whorls of dark hair. She was mesmerised by the sight of his hand lightly circling himself, moving lazily, biding his time until she could pleasure him.

'I'd rather *you* were doing this…'

Violet made her way over to him so that she was within touching distance…within licking distance…

Damien groaned and flung his head back, eyes closed, enjoying her tongue and mouth on him. He curled his hands into her hair, cupping her head. He had to steel himself against a powerful urge to let go, to release himself. He was in the process of physically losing control and he almost failed to recognise that fact because it was not something with which he was familiar. For him, making love had always been a finely tuned art form, where mutual pleasure rose along a predictable, albeit pleasurable, incline.

With a shudder, he reluctantly pulled her away from him and took a few seconds to gather himself.

Violet experienced a heady feeling of power. That this beautiful, desirable alpha male had to steady himself because of her…

She revelled in the unusual situation of really and truly, for the first time in her life, letting herself go. She felt as though she had had years of always having to be the one in control. Even in her one and only relationship, she had remained that person—the person who always thought before acting, the person who was always responsible. In giving Phillipa permission to be exactly the person she wanted to be, Violet, without knowing it, had tailored her own responses, had become the one who held back because *someone* had to, in the absence of parents.

Now…

She licked his rigid shaft once again and felt the roughness of veins against her tongue, a contrast to the silky smoothness at the top.

She had a moment's hesitation as her ever present common sense cranked into gear.

What was going on here? So yes, he was an intensely attractive man. It was perfectly understandable that she might be attracted to him. Attraction and lust had nothing to do with love and affection. She knew that now. But why on earth did *he* find *her* attractive? He was a man used to supermodels. She had seen pictures of them and, on his own admission, his first impressions of her had hardly been positive. So was he here now because a certain amount of boredom had met a similar amount of curiosity and the two, in this strangely charged situation, had combined to produce desire? Had the charade of playing their respective parts spilled over into reality?

For whatever reason, this man wanted her and for even more nebulous reasons, and against her better judgement, she wanted him. She knew what she should do. But suddenly she thought of her sister, flitting around in Ibiza, doing exactly what she wanted to do while she, Violet, remained behind to pick up the pieces. She thought of herself, always travelling in the slow lane, always taking care, while the fast-paced rush of the unexpected and the novel flew past her, leaving her in its wake.

Why, she wondered with a spurt of rebellion, shouldn't *she* jump on the roller coaster for once in her life? Why should she hold back at this eleventh hour? Would it be fair to herself? It certainly wouldn't be fair to *him*.

So what they had wouldn't last but what did she stand to lose? Damien meant nothing to her emotionally. He turned her on but she would always be able to walk away from lust because, sooner or later, her common sense would once again kick in, telling her that it was time to move on. When that time came, she would get back out there and jump back into the dating game, find herself a nice guy. She would never look back and have regrets that she had had her one window to be reckless and she had chosen to primly shut it and walk away.

She raised her head to meet his eyes and read the naked desire there.

'You're fabulous,' he said roughly, and Violet smiled and blushed because she couldn't think of a time when anyone had called her that.

'You're just saying that…'

'Don't tell me you haven't driven your fair share of men crazy before…' He raised himself, pulled her towards him and kissed her with driving urgency, stifling any confirmation. He didn't want to think of her with any other man. It was an unsettling and momentary pull of possessiveness that was completely alien to him.

His mouth never left hers as he found one breast and massaged its plumpness, finding the erect peak of her nipple to tease it until she was squirming.

In shocking detail, his voice rough and uneven, he told her exactly what he wanted to do with her, where he wanted to touch her, what he wanted her to feel.

Violet's skin burned hotly with the thrill of what he was saying. True, her experience when it came to the opposite sex was limited to one guy, but even so nothing could quite have prepared her for this sensory overload. His husky sex talk was doing all sorts of things in her mind while his hand, which had moved from her breast to caress the fluffy downy hair between her legs, was having a similar effect on her body.

She writhed and moaned softly, lowering herself to rake her teeth along his shoulder. He flipped her over so that he was now on top of her and she watched the progress of his dark head as he trailed a blazing path with his mouth along her shoulders to clamp on her nipple. Her nails dug into his shoulder blades then moved to tangle into his hair so that she could urge his mouth harder on her sensitised nipple.

He told her to tell him what she liked. Violet blushed furiously and thought that that was something she would never be able to do in a million years.

'So…' Damien was inordinately thrilled at her shyness. On so many levels he had been spot on when he had told her that she made a refreshing change. He had raised himself up now, his powerful body over hers, his hardness pressed against her, which made her desperate to open her legs and guide him inside. He laughed when she tried and told her that he was having none of that. Yet.

'You don't talk during sex…' He slipped two fingers inside her, felt her wetness and began teasing her, rubbing the throbbing little bud of her clitoris until she was gasping, only to move his attention elsewhere so that she didn't peak.

'Damien…'

'How do you expect me to know what turns you on if you don't tell me…?'

'You *know* what turns me on… You're…you're…'

'Doing it right now?'

'Please…'

'I like it that you're begging me…do you enjoy it when *I* talk…?' He whispered a few more things in her ear and Violet groaned. 'Well…?' His exploring fingers drove deeper inside her and she tightened her legs.

'Yes,' Violet whispered, then she shot him a devilish smile, 'although right now…there's other stuff I'd like you to do…'

'Tell me…'

'I…I can't…' She felt as green as a virgin.

'Of course you can,' Damien coaxed. It was taking a massive amount of willpower to maintain this leisurely pace. Her body pressed against his was beyond a turn-on and the slippery wetness between her legs was something he could barely think about because, if he did, he knew that he would lose control.

'I like it when you…suck my nipples…they're very sensitive…' Violet could feel her skin burning as though she was on fire. She felt forward and wanton and thoroughly debauched and she wondered how it was that she had never, ever been tempted to let go like this before. For a second she panicked at the notion that a man with whom she had nothing in common had been the one to rouse her to these heights.

'Your wish is my command…and I have other things in store for you…'

Violet decided not to think. She immersed herself in sensation after sensation as he suckled on her nipples, his tongue darting and rubbing and licking and then she gasped, shocked, as his wandering mouth travelled southwards. When she stammered that she had never…he couldn't possibly mean to…he laughed, deep-throated and amused, and proceeded to precisely what she had never…

His head between her legs made her want to cry out loud. Of their own volition, they parted to accommodate his ministrations and he was very thorough. He teased her with his tongue until she knew that she couldn't stand it any longer, then he angled his big body so that she could pleasure him just as he was pleasuring her.

Her legs were spread wide as he continued to feast on her. His tongue probed every bit of her and she did likewise to him, taking his bigness into her mouth, tasting it in every way possible. Only when she knew that they were both about to tip over the edge did he raise himself up, pulling apart only to ask her if she was protected. He was breathing heavily.

Why on earth would she be? Violet wanted to ask. But she knew that, for Damien, his relationships would always have been with women who travelled prepared. She was certain that had they fallen into bed in his house or flat or apartment, or wherever it was he lived, there would be ample supplies of condoms in a bedside cabinet. She shook her head. She searched his face for signs of impatience and frustration but there were none. Instead, he rubbed himself against her and murmured that full intercourse would have to wait.

'There are other ways to keep busy...'

Violet was lost for words at his generosity. She wasn't completely naive. She knew that a lot of men would have been angry, enraged even, to have had their pleasure curtailed, even if it wasn't the woman's fault. A lot of men were selfish. Contrary to first impressions, Damien clearly was not one of those men.

Something shifted inside her but it was something she didn't stop to analyse. Just at that moment, her brain wasn't up to doing anything analytical. Not when he was touching her once again, burying his head between her thighs, relentlessly teasing her throbbing clitoris with his tongue.

Their bodies seemed to fuse into one and when, finally, she climaxed, thrusting up against his greedy mouth, she felt utterly spent. She blindly reached for him, felt his hardness and curved her languorous body so that her mouth met it, so that she could take him to the same heights to which he had taken her.

Their bodies were slick with perspiration and the room filled with the miasma of sex. He tugged her off him before he came and she felt his ejection on her face and body. It mirrored her own wetness that glistened on his face. When they kissed as he returned to Planet Earth, it was the most sensuous thing she had ever done. She felt giddy from such complete loss of her self-control.

'I think tomorrow we might pay a visit to the chemist…' Damien was on top of the world. What was it about this woman? They hadn't even indulged in full intercourse and why kid himself, no amount of inventive touching could compare to the unique sensation of penetration. Yet he was infused with a feeling of absolute well-being. On a high. He wanted to start all over again, touching, tracing her body with his hands, tasting…

He pulled her against him and relished the softness of her full breasts squashed against his chest.

'I don't know how this happened…'

'Are you saying you wish it hadn't?'

'No,' Violet admitted truthfully, 'but I'm not the kind of girl who falls into bed with men…'

'Not even with the boyfriend you happen to be deeply in love with?'

It took a couple of seconds for it to register that he was teasing her. 'Ha, ha, very funny…' she said weakly. *But what happens next?* she wanted to ask. Except the question seemed strangely inappropriate.

'This complicates things…' she said instead.

It was precisely why he had made such a big effort not to go there. Even when he had acknowledged that he was attracted to her, even though he was a man who had never missed a step between attraction and possession, it was precisely why Damien had stepped back. Because he had acknowledged that to sleep with her would be to complicate an already complicated situation.

Now, with her sexy, luscious body pressed against his, there was no room in his head for thoughts of complications.

'That's one way of looking at it. On the other hand, you could say that it makes the situation much more interesting.'

'I'm not an interesting person.'

'Leave the character assessment to me…' He smoothed his hand over her thigh, slipped it underneath, sandwiching it between her legs, his own personal hand warmer.

Violet knew exactly what sort of character assessment he was talking about. It had nothing to do with her personality.

'So we're here…and we're sleeping together. You might say it adds a great deal more veracity to the situation. No need to pretend…'

Except, Violet thought, they were *still* pretending. Pretending an emotional connection that was absent, even though there was now a physical one.

'You're still frowning.'

'I can't help it.'

'Live for the present.'

'I've never been good at doing that. When our parents died, I was left in charge of Phillipa and the last thing I could afford to do was live for the present.'

'I get that,' Damien murmured. He wasn't one for soul-searching conversations but he was feeling incredibly relaxed. 'With a sister like her, you had to carry worries about the future for both of you.' He gently parted her legs and slipped his finger along the crease that protected her femininity like the petals of a flower.

'I can't…talk when you're doing that…'

'Fine by me. Touching and talking don't go hand in hand. At least…not unless the talking's dirty…which I've discovered turns you on…'

'But we have to talk…'

'Wouldn't you rather…'

'Damien!' She could feel her body tensing and building up to a climax. His caressing hand was doing all sorts of things to her and yet there was stuff that needed to be said.

'I know. Irresistible, isn't it? And you can feel how much it's turning me on as well…'

Violet wondered how it would be were they to make love fully, properly… Her imagination soared as the rubbing movements against the pulsating bud of her clitoris got faster and faster and when she came it was an explosion that left her drained.

She curled against him. 'What happens now…?' She hadn't wanted to pose the question but it was one that needed to be asked.

Damien stilled. Questions of that nature always left him cold. However, in a strange way, this was a far more straightforward situation. 'You come up next weekend. As agreed. But I won't be working till one in the morning and leaving the bedroom by six. It has to be said that the prospect of sojourns in the countryside has taken on a distinctly upbeat tempo.'

'But I'm not your real girlfriend…'

'Where are you going with this?'

'Do we communicate during the week?' She worried her lower lip as she tried to get her head round a relationship that wasn't a relationship. 'Or do we just become involved when we're here? I mean,' she added, just in case he got it into his head she would spend Monday to Friday pining for his company and putting her life on hold, 'what if I meet someone…? I have quite a busy social life. Teachers like going out after school. Most of us feel we need a drink after a day in the company of high energy kids.'

'Meet someone?' He shifted so that he could look down at her.

'I've been thinking about getting back into the dating scene. For some reason, it's always been difficult with Phillipa around. I guess she just took up so much of my energy. I spent so much time worrying about what she was getting up to and listening to her personal sagas that there never seemed to be much time left over for myself. With Phillipa in Ibiza now…'

Damien's brain had come to a screeching halt at the words *getting back into the dating scene.* They had just made love! He was outraged. How could she even be contemplating the prospect of some other guy when she was lying next to him, her body still hot and flushed after her climax that he had given her?

'Sorry, but that's not going to happen.' He flung himself back and stared up at the ceiling with its ornate mouldings which he could hardly make out in the darkness. He felt her shift next to him so that she, likewise, was staring up at the ceiling.

'I'm not following you…'

'Explain to me how, on the one hand, you say that you don't climb into bed with random men whilst on the other telling me that you want to start going to nightclubs and sleeping with whoever takes your fancy at the time…'

'That's not at all what I said!'

'No? It sounded very much like that to me. And I am very much offended that you would even think of raising a subject of this nature after we've spent the past hour and a half making love. In fact, you shouldn't even be *thinking* about other men. Right now, *I* should be the only man on your mind.'

'The game's changed,' Violet said calmly on a deep breath, 'and now there are different rules.'

'Enlighten me.'

'Why do you have to be so arrogant?'

'It's one of the more endearing aspects of my personality. You were going to tell me about these new rules.'

'I... For some weird reason I find I'm attracted to you.' She took a deep breath. 'You've told me that I should live in the present and I guess this is my one-off opportunity to do that. I never expected it to happen, but there you go.'

'So...other guys...out of the question. Nightclubs and sex after two drinks...likewise out of the question.'

'In which case, the same rules apply to you.'

Damien rolled to his side and looked at her. In accordance with a serious conversation, she had tucked the duvet right up to her neck.

'Gladly.' He pulled the duvet down, exposing her breasts and he gently nuzzled a rosy tip until it stiffened against his tongue. 'Gladly?' Violet tugged him up so that he was looking at her, although her body was aching for him to carry on doing what it had been doing so well.

'I'm a one woman kind of man...'

Violet wondered whether that was because he happened to be temporarily stuck far away from the action but then she conceded that, however arrogant and infuriating he could be, his ground rules would be fair.

'And besides...' he nibbled her lower lip, tugging it gently between his teeth '...this works...'

'You said you first thought that getting involved like this...'

'Falling into bed together and making love until we're too exhausted to move…'

'…would complicate things.' Violet didn't know what she wanted him to say. She had knowingly thrown caution to the winds and yet she still felt confused. She had never felt so physically satisfied—*never ever*—and yet the road ahead still seemed opaque and clouded with uncertainty. He might not want to put a label to what they now had, but effectively they were an item. For real. And yet why didn't it feel that way? And did she really expect him to set those niggling anxieties to rest?

'I wasn't thinking out of the box. I've found that women seem to associate fun in bed with meeting the parents and eventually shopping for a wedding ring. You…' seemingly of its own volition, his hand caressed her breast; he couldn't get enough of her '…fall into a different category. You know how the ground lies. I'm not looking for any kind of commitment. Been there, done that, won't be revisiting that particular holiday hotspot in the foreseeable future. But what's going on right now…mind-blowing…and I'm not one to throw around superlatives lightly…' He shot her a smouldering smile that made her toes curl. 'I won't be casting my net anywhere else and, if it makes you happy, you can communicate with me all you want to during the week. In fact, you'll need to be updated on my mother's progress. I'm sure she'll also get in touch. It would be abnormal for you to be ignorant of how she is doing. So I'm guessing all your questions have been sorted…'

They were having fun. Plus it was convenient. But he was trusting her not to get emotionally wrapped up. When he said that they would communicate during the week, she knew that their conversations would be about Eleanor, that there would be a specific reason for them to happen in the first place. They wouldn't be passing the time chatting about nothing much in particular. Violet decided that she was fine with that. She had never been the sort of person who kept the various sections of her life neatly boxed away and separated. This was how it was done. Of course, it would take a little getting used to but she would do it because, like it or not, she was greedy for the physical exhilaration he had introduced into her life, which, on that level, now seemed bland and nondescript in comparison.

She parted her legs and felt his hardness rub against her. No penetration but the sensation produced was still powerful and she moved in time to increase the pressure.

'And when things fizzle out between us…' she volunteered breathlessly.

'It's called the natural course of events.'

She could hardly imagine him being so deeply in love with a woman that he would want to take it to the very limit, that he would propose marriage. She couldn't get her head around the notion of him offering commitment rather than talking about the natural course of events. For a man as intensely proud and intensely passionate, she could understand how he could have been permanently damaged by the most significant relationship in his life going belly up. Eleanor had never broached the subject of Annalise again and neither had she. Damien's past was none of her business. This was the here and now. Everything he said made sense. This was her one opportunity to ditch her comfort zone and there was no point having a mental debate on the pros and cons of the clauses attached.

'We'll go our separate ways but as long as we're lovers you'll find, my darling, that I am exceedingly generous…'

'Your money doesn't mean anything to me.' She tried not to feel hurt at the implication that she could be shoved into the predictable mould of one of his women, eager to take whatever gifts were on offer. 'That's not why…I don't care if you own the Bank of England. I don't want anything from you.'

Damien thought that whilst she might say that now, her tune would change the second he presented her with her very first diamond-encrusted bracelet or top-of-the-range sports car.

'Frankly, my mother would expect it.'

'She already knows that I'm not the materialistic kind.'

'More confidences exchanged during one of your cosy tête-à-têtes?' But he liked her protestations of wholesomeness. What guy in his position wouldn't? Even if, sooner or later, the moral high ground took a bit of a beating? Greed and avarice were frequent visitors to his life. It was nice not to have them knocking on the door just yet.

'We don't *just* talk about you!'

'I'm hurt. I thought I was never far from your thoughts…' He moved fractionally against her and she squirmed and her eyes fluttered. To stop herself from losing control altogether once again, she reached down and firmly held him in her hand. The steel thickness of his girth made her shudder with wicked pleasure.

'You're not *in* my thoughts,' Violet denied vigorously. Having someone in your thoughts implied a *connection*. Even jokingly, she didn't want to go there, didn't want to let him think that he might be anything more to her than she was to him. 'You crop up in conversation with your mother because you're the person we have in common and, under normal circumstances, a girlfriend would be really happy to hear her stories about the guy in her life from his mother. It's natural that your mother would want to talk about you. Now, though, we talk about other things. Art, the garden, life in a small community, the treatment and what it might involve…and I don't just have conversations with your mother. I talk a lot to Dominic as well. He has a lot to say. You just have to be patient. He gets frustrated because he can't communicate as fluently as he'd like, but he's smart.'

Damien gently removed her hand from him. Reluctantly. Of course, warning bells shouldn't be ringing. They were, after all, singing from the same song sheet but still...just in case...

'Don't get too wrapped up, Violet.'

'What do you mean?'

'I mean...we might become more involved with one another than either of us anticipated or probably even wanted, and your role might have been extended beyond what I envisaged, but don't start nurturing ideas of permanence.'

'I wouldn't do that!' She pulled away from him. 'And you don't have to warn me! You've already made the parameters of what we have perfectly clear. I understand, Damien. It suits me! I'm not an idiot.'

'But you're forming links with my family,' Damien said drily.

'I'm *having conversations*!' But she could detect the coolness in his voice. This wasn't a gentle caution. This was a warning shot across the bows, a blunt reminder that she was not to go beyond the Keep Out signs he had erected around himself. If she did, and the message was clear though unspoken, she would be ditched. He would enjoy her but that was as far as things would go. In short, *don't start getting any ideas...*

'I'm a big girl. I know how to take care of myself. And because the women you've dated in the past might have wanted more from you than you were prepared to give, that's not the case with me. I've always been careful. I'm just having a go at what it feels like not to be careful for once in my life. And do you always have a list prepared of dos and don'ts when you start a...something? With a woman? Or is this specially for me because I happen to have met your family?'

Violet knew that she shouldn't be pursuing this. This wasn't part of her decision to *be daring for once in her life*.

'I'm always upfront when it comes to women. I let them know that I'm not in it for the long-term.'

'Because you've been hurt once doesn't mean that you have to spend the rest of your life keeping your distance.'

'Come again?' Damien said coldly.

'I'm sorry. I shouldn't have said that.' But had he laid down loads of rules and regulations for Annalise? No. She wasn't in the same category—of course she wasn't—but neither did she need to be subjected to a hundred and one boundary lines because he thought she was too gullible or too stupid to know how the land lay.

'Let's move on from this conversation, Violet. My past is not fertile ground for discussion.' And he was willing to let it go. His magnanimity surprised him because he categorically did not invite anyone's opinions on certain aspects of his life. Naturally, he didn't want to engineer an argument. He hadn't enjoyed the past few days of awkwardness. And also, for once, he was thinking with that part of his body which he always had under control. Never had elemental desire been so important a factor in his response.

'As I said, I understand the parameters and it suits me.'

'You're using me, in other words.' His voice was light and amused.

'No more than you're using me.'

Not quite the response he had expected. He gave a low laugh. Fair's fair, he thought. Wasn't it? He'd never had any woman admit to using him before. So what if the feeling didn't sit *quite right*? He wanted her. She wanted him. Trim away the excess and that was all that mattered.

CHAPTER EIGHT

DAMIAN REACHED INTO his jacket pocket and flipped open the lid of the black and gold box which had been nestling there for the past three hours.

A necklace with a teardrop pendant, a blood-red ruby, surrounded by tiny diamonds. He had chosen it himself. Well, why not? Suitable recompense for the past three and a half months, during which Violet had proved herself a superb and satisfying lover. He always gave gifts to his lovers. She might have thwarted every attempt he had made thus far on that front, rebutting his offers of a car, *because who needed to become snarled up in traffic, not to mention contributing to global warming whilst having to pay the Congestion Charge the second you needed it for anything really useful?* an expensive weekend in Vienna now that his mother seemed to be responding so well to her treatment programme, *can't, too much work, sorry,* some really expensive kitchen equipment because he had seen what she had, *no, thanks, a girl becomes accustomed to working with old, familiar pots and pans and ovens and fridges and microwaves...*

But this necklace was a fait accompli. She would have no choice but to accept it.

He snapped shut the lid of the box and returned it to

his jacket pocket before sliding out of his car and heading up to her house.

He had grown accustomed to the confined space in which she lived. Literally two-up, two-down. Phillipa was still doing whatever she was doing in Ibiza. He couldn't imagine the claustrophobia of actually having to share the place with another adult human being. Personally, it would have driven him mad. He was used to the vast open-plan space of his five-bedroom house in Chelsea. When he had moved there years ago, he had hired a top architect who had re-configured the layout of the house so that the rooms, all painted stone and adorned with a mixture of established art and newer investment worthy pieces, flowed into one another.

Violet's house was more in the nature of a honeycomb. Two weeks previously, he had offered to have the whole thing gutted and redone more along his tastes, but predictably she had looked at him as though he had taken leave of his senses and laughed. Alternatively, he had said, they could just spend more time at his place. He was now splitting his time between London and the West Country. Why not make love in luxury? But she had told him, in the sort of semi-apologetic voice that managed to impart no hint of remorse, that she didn't like his house. Something about it being sterile and clinical. He had refrained from telling her that she was the first woman to have ever responded to opulence with a negative reaction.

He pressed the doorbell and instantly lost his train of thought at the sound of her approaching footsteps.

From inside the house, Violet felt that familiar shiver of tingling, excited anticipation. After the first month, and once he had ascertained that Eleanor was responding well, Damien had split his time. He always made sure to spend weekends in the country and often Mondays as well, but he was now in London a great deal more and Violet liked that. On all levels, what she was doing was bad for her. She knew that. She didn't understand where this driving, urgent chemistry between them had sprung from and even less did she understand how it was capable of existing in a vacuum the way it did, but she was powerless to fight it. Having always equated sex with love, she had fast learned how easy it was for everything you took for granted to be turned inside out and upside down.

She had also fast learned how easy it was to lose track of the rules of the game you had signed up to.

When had she started living her week in anticipation of seeing him? Just when had she sacrificed all her principles, all her expectations of what a relationship should deliver on the high altar of lust and passion and sex?

She had told herself that she was throwing caution to the winds. That most of her adult years had been spent being responsible and diligent and careful so why on earth shouldn't she take a little time out and experience something else, something that wasn't all wrapped up with *doing the right thing*? She had practically decided that she *owed* herself that. That she was a grown woman who was more than capable of handling a sexual relationship with a man to whom she was inexplicably but powerfully attracted.

So how was it that it was now so difficult to maintain the mask of not caring one jot if he never discussed anything beyond tomorrow? If he assumed that whatever they had would fizzle out at some point? More and more she found herself thinking about Annalise, the wife that should have been but never was. He never mentioned her name. That in itself was telling because three weeks ago, on one of their rare excursions out for a meal at a swanky restaurant in Belgravia, he had bumped into a woman and had afterwards told her that he had dated her for a few months. The woman had been a flame-haired six-foot beauty, as slender as a reed and draped over a man much shorter and older. Afterwards, Damien had laughed and informed her that the man in question was a Russian billionaire, married but with his wife safely tucked away in the bowels of St Petersburg somewhere.

'Don't you feel a twinge of jealousy that he's dating a woman you used to go out with?' Violet had asked, because how could any man not? When the woman in question looked as though she had stepped straight off the front cover of a high-end fashion magazine? Damien had laughed. Why on earth would he be jealous? Women came and went. Good luck to the guy, although he had enough money to keep the lady in question amused and interested.

'Was she too expensive for you?' Violet had asked, which he had found even more amusing.

'No one's too expensive for me. I dumped her because she wanted more than money could buy.'

Violet had thought that that had said it all. The woman in question had wanted a ring on her finger. Damien, on the other hand, had wanted casual. Which was what he wanted with her and the only woman to whom those rules had never applied was the one woman who had broken his heart.

And yet, knowing all that, she could still feel herself sliding further and further away from logic, common sense and self-control. Forewarned wasn't forearmed.

She pulled open the door and her heart gave that weird skippy feeling, as though she were in a lift that had suddenly dropped a hundred floors at maximum speed.

It was Thursday and he had come straight from work, although his tie was missing and his jacket was slung over his shoulder.

'Damien...'

'Missed me?' Deep blue, hooded eyes swept over her with masculine appreciation. No bra. Ages ago, he had told her that it was an entirely unnecessary item of clothing for a woman whose breasts were as perfect as hers. At least indoors. When *he* was the male caller in question...

He had been leaning indolently against the doorframe. Now he pushed himself off and entered the tiny hallway, his eyes glued to her the whole time.

His smile was slow and lazy. With an easy movement, he tossed his jacket aside, where it landed neatly on the banister, then he wrapped his arms around her, drew her to him so that he could try and extinguish some of the yearning that had been building inside him from the very second he had set foot in his car. Her mouth parted readily and he grunted with pleasure as his tongue found hers, clashing in a hungry need for more.

Violet braced her hands against his chest and stayed him for a few seconds. 'You know I hate it when the first thing you do the very second you walk through the front door is...is...'

'Kiss you senseless...?' Damien raked his fingers through his hair. Frankly, he wasn't too fond of that particular trait himself. He didn't like what it said about his self-control when he was around her, but he chose to keep that to himself. 'Is that why the last time I came, we didn't even manage to make it up the stairs?' he said instead. 'In fact, if I recall...your jumper was off on stair two, I had your nipple in my mouth by stair four and by stair eight, roughly halfway up, I was exploring other parts of your extremely responsive body...'

Violet blushed. As always, it was one thing saying something and another actually putting it into practice.

Right now, although he had done as asked and had

drawn back from her, the one thing she wanted to do was pull him right back towards her so that they could carry on where they had left off.

It was only a very small consolation that these little shows of strength helped her to maintain the façade of being as casual about what they had as he was. She knew that she had to cling to them for dear life.

'I'm going to cook us something special.' She led the way to the kitchen and retrieved a cold bottle of beer from the fridge, which he took, tilting his head back to drink a couple of long mouthfuls.

'Why?'

Violet contained a little spurt of irritation. Shows of domesticity were never appreciated. He had never said so but, tellingly, his chef would often prepare food, which he would bring with him, stuff that tasted delicious and required an oven, a microwave and plates, or else takeaways were ordered when they had been physically sated. The ritual of eating was usually just an interruption, she sometimes felt, to the main event.

'I'm trying it out as a meal for my class to learn,' she lied and he shrugged and swallowed a couple more mouthfuls of beer before retreating to the kitchen table, where he sprawled on one chair, pulling another closer and using it as a footrest.

Violet bustled. Now that they weren't tripping over themselves, tearing each other's clothes off in a frantic race to make love, she wished that they were. Her body tingled at the knowledge that he was looking at her. She loved it when his eyes got dark and slumberous and full of intent.

'Tell me how your mother's doing,' she said, to clear her head from the wanton desire to fling herself at him and forget about the meal she had planned.

She listened as he told her about recent trips into the

village, her upbeat mood, which so contrasted with her despair when she had initially told him about the situation, recovery that was exceeding the doctor's expectations…

Violet half listened. Her mind was drifting in and out of the uncomfortable questions she had recently started asking herself. Occasionally she said something and hoped for the best. She was a million miles away when she jumped as Damien padded up towards her and whispered into her ear, 'Must be a complicated recipe, Violet. You've been staring into space for the past five minutes.'

Violet snapped back to the present and turned to him with a little frown. 'I've got stuff on my mind.'

'Anything I'd like to hear about?'

She hesitated, torn between not wanting to rock the boat and needing to say what she was thinking.

'No. Just to do with school.' She cravenly shied away from doing what she knew would ruin the evening.

'What can I do to take your mind off it…?' Just like that, Damien felt his tension evaporate. He thought he might have been imagining the thickness of the atmosphere, her unusual silence. He turned her back to the chopping board, where she had been mixing a satay sauce, and wrapped his arms around her from behind. 'Looks good. What is it?' He slipped one big hand underneath her loose top and did what he had been wanting to the moment he had set foot through the front door. He caressed one full breast, settling on a nipple, which he rubbed gently but insistently with the pad of his thumb. With his other hand, he dipped a finger into the sauce, licked some off and offered the rest to her. Violet's mouth circled round his finger and she shivered at the deliberate eroticism in the gesture.

She moved across to the kitchen sink, carrying some dishes with her, and he released her, but only briefly, before resuming his position standing right behind her.

Outside, with the days getting longer, darkness was only now beginning to set in. Her view was spectacularly unexciting. The back of the house overlooked the wall of another house; the outside space comprised of a pocket-sized back garden just big enough for Phillipa to lie down in summer and spend the day tanning without having to dismantle the washing line.

Their bodies, merging together, were reflected hazily back to them in the windows overlooking the garden and their eyes tangled in the reflection as he slowly pushed up her jumper until she could see both their bodies and the pale nudity of her breasts. She gasped and fell back slightly against him as he began massaging them, rhythmic, firm movements that pushed them up, making her large nipples bulge and distend.

'Damien…no…someone might see us…' Although that wasn't really a possibility. The one thing about the house and its location was that it was surprisingly private, given the fact that it was in London, where privacy was a rarity. The small back garden was fully enclosed with a fence and a fortuitous tree in the back garden of the neighbour opposite ensured limited view.

Damien continued rubbing her breasts, filling his hands with the heavy weight of them, bouncing them slightly, as though evaluating their worth.

'Get naked for me,' he murmured, nipping her neck and then trailing hot kisses along it.

'Get…what…?'

'Don't pretend you didn't hear. Get naked for me. Take your clothes off. Scratch that. Maybe I'll let you get away with just wearing an apron…'

'I'm not dressing up for your enjoyment!' But already the thought of his dark, intense eyes following her naked body as she moved around the kitchen was making her feel hot and bothered.

'I'm not asking you to dress up. I'm asking you to dress down...' He shifted her jumper up, over her breasts, and Violet responded by spinning round to face him, her bare breasts pushing against the hard wall of his chest.

She began unbuttoning his shirt. From a position of relative inexperience only months ago, she had grown in confidence. He might not have had it at his disposal to offer anything most women would have expected of a proper relationship, but he certainly had it within him to turn her into a woman who was no longer tentative when it came to responding in ways that would pleasure her.

She shoved her hands under his shirt and felt the abrasive rub of his chest, not smooth and androgynous, but aggressively masculine with its dark hair. Slowly, she pushed the shirt off his broad shoulders, running her hands expertly along the contours of his muscles until the shirt had joined her jumper on the kitchen floor.

He propped himself against the counter, caging her in, and took his time kissing her until her whole body was burning up and she could feel the damp heat pooling between her legs.

'Those jogging bottoms do nothing at all for your superb figure... They should be banned from your wardrobe...' He slipped his fingers underneath the stretchy waistband and tugged them down, allowing her to wriggle out of them, keeping his arms on either side of her so that her movements were restricted. When he looked down, he could see her generous breasts shifting as she moved, soft and succulent. Unable to resist, he captured one and lifted it until her nipple was pouting directly at him. Reluctantly he decided that a full-on assault would have to wait. He wanted to take his time. She had been in his head for days; frankly, from the last time he had seen her, which had been the previous week, and he wasn't going to rush things. He had spent hours fantasising about the next time they met and he intended to see at least some of those fantasies translated into sexy reality.

'Same goes for the underwear…'

'But it's beautiful lacy underwear…' Violet protested with mock hurt. 'Brand new! And very expensive…not the sort of underwear a hard-working teacher can afford too much of…'

'I'll buy you the store. Then you can save your hard-earned salary for other things…'

Violet traced the outline of his flat brown nipples, moistened her fingers with her tongue, traced them again, and relished the way he flexed in immediate, gratifying response.

'I like the underwear,' Damien asserted huskily as he looked down at the lacy lavender piece of nothing. 'I just don't like it on you at this particular moment in time…' He pointedly tugged the lace, then, without giving her time to protest, knelt in front of her.

Looking down with a little gasp, Violet saw the dark bowed head of a supplicant. Even if he was very far from being one. It was an incredible turn-on.

He gently urged her thighs slightly apart and then peeled the underwear back, revealing the lushness of her hair.

With a shudder, she braced herself against the counter, head flung back, knowing that if she wasn't careful she would come in seconds. As his tongue slipped into the groove of her wetly receptive sex, she could hear the faint slick sounds as he licked and explored, with his finger still holding the underwear to one side.

She clenched her fists and gritted her teeth in a mammoth effort not to come against his questing mouth.

She reached down to tug his hair and, on cue, he straightened. Her hands scrabbled helplessly at his trousers and he gave a deep throaty laugh and began to unzip them.

'We haven't made it to the food,' he murmured.

'But at least we're not on the staircase…' As if that said anything, as if it implied any more restraint. It didn't. She was as desperate for him now as she always was when he came through her door.

'No. The kitchen. Lots of scope for being inventive… although would you rather we ate the food than tried playing with it…?' Damien laughed at her shocked expression. She had only had one other lover. He had managed to get that out of her ages ago and, from the sounds of it, that one lover had hardly been sizzling in the bedroom stakes. Every time they made love, he felt as though he was coming to her as her first and the feeling that generated was beyond satisfaction. 'Okay,' he drawled, 'maybe next time. I could teach you some very inventive things that can be done with champagne and cherries…'

He removed his trousers and underwear in one smooth movement. The kitchen was warm and fragrant with the food that had already started cooking. Outside, night had finally drawn in. With the lights off, they were just two shadows touching, feeling and responding to one another.

He breathed in her uniquely feminine scent, something to do with a light floral perfume she wore. It wouldn't have suited everyone but it damn well suited her. Even when they were apart, he could recall the smell and it always managed to get him aroused. How was that possible? He half closed his eyes and was relieved that she couldn't witness that momentary lapse of self-control.

For a few seconds a streak of anger flared inside him. A confused, chaotic anger that resented the peculiar hold he sometimes thought she had over him. He lifted her, taking her by surprise, and sat her on the counter, shoving aside the remnants of food and cutlery still to be cleared.

'What are you doing?' Violet's voice was breathless as her rear made contact with the cool surface of the kitchen counter.

'I'm taking you.'

'But…'

He didn't say anything, instead holding her with one hand while he bent to retrieve the wallet from his trousers, home of at least one extremely useful condom if memory served him right. He was hard and erect, throbbing with an urgent need to sink into her body and feel it wrap itself around him like a glove.

Her hands were on his shoulders and her short pearly nails were digging into his flesh. Leaning back, her breasts were thrust out, nipples standing to attention. He paused briefly to take one into his mouth, sucking hard on it until she was whimpering and crying out and could no longer keep still. His leisurely lovemaking plan had taken a nose-dive. Pushing open her legs and angling her just right so that she was ready to receive him, he entered her.

Pleasure exploded in her like a thunderbolt. She could feel every magnificent inch of him as he moved inside her, strong, forceful and with deepening intensity.

This was almost rough and yet it felt so good. She heard herself crying out and the sound seemed to be coming from someone else.

'Talk to me!' he demanded, curling his long fingers into her hair, tugging her into looking at him. Which she did, through half closed eyes because she was pretty much beyond focusing on anything but what he was doing to her.

'Damien!' He talked dirty to her but it was something she had not done in return. Some lingering element of prudishness always seemed to stand in the way.

'Tell me how you're feeling with me inside you!' He emphasised the order with a powerful thrust that made her slide a little way back on the counter.

Violet shivered with heady abandon. She clutched him and told him exactly what he was demanding to know. How it felt to have him in her, filling her up, taking away her ability to think. Her breasts ached for him. She wanted his mouth on them. She just couldn't get enough of him...

To her own ears, every word she uttered seemed to plunge her deeper and deeper into a vulnerable place. Would he pick that up? Was that finely tuned instinct of his sharp enough to pick up what wasn't being said behind the graphic descriptions? That she literally couldn't get enough of him, and not just on the physical, carnal plane, addictive though that was? That, for her, want was very much interlinked with need, which was dangerously close to...

Violet clamped shut her mouth, allowed herself to be carried away to oblivion. She cried out mindlessly as wave upon wave of glorious, unstoppable sensation ripped through her perspiring body, and he echoed her.

When he withdrew from her, turning to deposit the used condom in the bin, she scrambled off the counter and, for a few seconds, barely remembered the train of thought that had been running through her head just before she had climaxed.

It was a luxury that wasn't destined to last long. She went upstairs for a quick shower. She desperately needed some time to herself, time for her thought processes to be followed through to their natural conclusion, even though the conclusion might not be one she wanted to reach.

She had fallen in love with him. How had that happened? Shouldn't there have been a natural progression of steps to get from A to B? Where was the calm, peaceful contentment she had always associated with falling in love? She had been swept along on a roller coaster ride and now she felt ambushed by an emotion that had crept in without her noticing, without her being able to take the necessary precautions. Whilst she had been racing with the devil and calling it *experience,* a *one-off,* love had been quietly settling like cement and now she felt constricted, unable to move and as fragile as a piece of spun glass.

She went downstairs to find that he had tidied the kitchen, which surely must have been a first for him, and waiting for her with a glass of wine in his hand. His trousers were back on, as was the shirt, although he hadn't bothered to do up the buttons on the shirt which hung rakishly loose, revealing a sliver of bronzed torso.

'Full marks for the appetiser...' Damien sipped some of his wine and regarded her over the rim of the glass. If she had used a shower cap, it hadn't done its job. Damp tendrils clung to her cheeks. She looked clean and rosy and unbelievably sexy, especially with the V-necked striped T-shirt she had put on, which allowed a generous view of her cleavage. It was a constant source of mystery that her appeal hadn't diminished over the course of time. Why was that? Was it because he was fully aware that they came from opposite ends of the pole? That, for a man like him—a man who didn't want commitment—he had found his match in a woman who probably *did* want commitment but not with a man like him? Could that be it?

Violet's eyes skittered away from his beautiful, sinfully sexy face. Every compliment he paid her had to do with sex, with her body, with the physical. She could see now that that had been the start of her downfall. Those husky words of rampant appreciation, delivered with intent, had arrowed in on a part of her that had always been insecure and found their mark. Like a flower coming into bloom, she had opened up and grown in an area of her life that had been stunted and underdeveloped. He had made her feel like a woman, a powerful, beautiful, engaging woman, and she had run with the sensation. She had let him in and, without even realising it, had seen beyond their differences to all the things about him that were strangely endearing.

'Damien…we need to…to talk…'

He continued to smile that crooked little half smile of his but his eyes were suddenly watchful. Women wanting *to talk* was usually synonymous with women *saying things he didn't want to hear.*

'I'm listening.' He strolled across to one of the kitchen chairs and sat down, looking at her carefully as she shuffled to the chair opposite him, so that the width of the table was separating them.

'It's been a while, Damien. Your mother has responded really well to treatment and is out of the danger zone. I agreed to all of this…pretending, the charade…for my sister and then I carried on with it for myself, because I was talked into putting sexual attraction above everything else…'

'Ah. I get it. Are we going to start on a blame game, Violet? With me cast in the role of seducer of innocent girls? If that's the case, then I suggest you have a rethink before you get on your soapbox.'

Violet had forgotten this side to him, the side that could withdraw and grow cold. The fact that it was still there, right beneath the surface, was a timely reminder of why it was so important to begin detaching herself from this relationship, if indeed relationship was what it could be called.

'I wasn't going to do that.'

'No?' Damien drawled. He hadn't been expecting this, not after having had mind-blowing sex, and tension lent a hard, mocking edge to his voice. 'Because no one pointed to a bed and then held a gun to your head while you got undressed.'

'I know that! Why are you being so…so horrible?'

'I'm just waiting to hear what you have to say and reminding you that you were an eager and willing volunteer when it came to sex.' She couldn't meet his eyes. What the hell was going on? How could everything change in a matter of seconds? His confusion angered him because it was yet another niggling reminder that he was not as much in control with this woman as he would have liked to have been.

'I'm saying that I think it would be a good idea if we… we…took a step back…' Violet lowered her eyes and frowned into the glass of wine which had somehow found its way in front of her.

'A step back…'

'Your mother is more than stable enough to deal with our relationship hitting the rocks. She's back to doing stuff with Dominic, can go out in her garden now and again… I feel that the time has come for us to get back to our normal lives…'

'And between us making love in the kitchen and you going to have a shower…you've reached this decision *when…? Exactly…?*'

'I don't have to give you any explanations of when or why I've reached my decision, Damien. It's over. I'm not like you. I can't carry on sleeping with you, knowing that it's something that's not going anywhere.'

'Where do you want it to go?' Damien asked, as quick as a flash.

'I don't want it to go anywhere!'

'And what if I tell you that I don't want what we have to end yet? Doubtless my mother is strong enough to recover from a crash and burn relationship, even if she's unduly fond of you, but it's long ceased to be about my mother, as you well know.' Suddenly restless, he vaulted to his feet, glass in one hand, and began to pace the tiny kitchen. He'd never been dumped by a woman. Pride alone should have had him gathering his jacket and heading for the door. Hadn't he made it his mission to avoid the hassle of the demanding woman? And what was she demanding anyway? She had always made it quite clear that they were poles apart, that he was not the blueprint of the kind of man she would ever consider settling down with.

So…was it money? Underneath all the protestations of not being materialistic, had she become used to the opulence that surrounded him wherever he went? Had she glimpsed a vision of how life could be if she could get access to his? He stifled a sudden feeling of intense disappointment. He was a realist and this was the explanation that made the most sense.

His brain locked into gear. He still wanted her and, whether she admitted it or not, she was still hot for him. So maybe she didn't feel as though she had a stake in their relationship. She made a big song and dance of not wanting to accept anything from him but, in so doing, did she feel that she was utterly disposable? That, despite his offers to buy her no less than he would have bought for any of his lovers, he found her in any way less attractive? If only… Just thinking about the way her breasts spilled heavily out of her bra was enough to engage his mind for a few seconds on a completely different path. If he had felt, in any way, that the sex was beginning to wane, he might have shrugged and taken his leave but he was an expert when it came to gauging responses. He couldn't remember a time when the woman had been the flagging partner and it wasn't the case now. Nor was he about to give up a sex life that was second to none.

'There's something I want you to see.'

Violet was taken aback by a remark that seemed to come from nowhere. 'What is it?'

'Wait here.' In the heat of the moment, he had forgotten the costly item of jewellery nestling in its classy black and gold box. His fait accompli present. Whoever said that the Great One didn't work in mysterious ways?

She was still sitting in the same position in the kitchen when he returned and extended his hand. 'For you,' he informed her solemnly. 'I hear what you're saying and this is just a small measure of what you mean to me...'

Violet took the box but already she could feel her skin beginning to get clammy. *What he meant to her.* How many times had she told him that she didn't want anything from him? She lifted the lid of the box and stared down at an item of jewellery that she knew would have been spectacularly expensive. What she meant to him would never be love, it certainly wasn't durability. She was his willing plaything and her worth could be counted in banknotes. She fought down the stupid urge to cry over a piece of jewellery that would have had any other woman shrieking in delight.

'I don't want it.' She stuck it back in the box, snapped shut the lid and handed it to him.

'What do you mean? I know you've made a big deal about not accepting anything from me, but you want to know what this...what we have...means to me...take it in the spirit with which it was given.' He obviously wasn't about to relieve her of the necklace.

'I think it's time we called this a day, Damien.' It hurt just saying that but say it she knew she had to. In that single gesture he had made her feel sordid and cheap.

'Where the hell is this coming from?'

'I can't be bought for a few weeks or months of sex

until you get tired of me and send me on my way with…
with *what*…? Something even bigger and more expensive? A really huge pat on the back, it was nice knowing
you goodbye gift?'

Damien wondered how long she had been contemplating the outcome of their relationship and working herself
up to wanting more. Was she holding him to ransom or
did she genuinely want out and if she did genuinely want
out, how was it that she was still on fire for him? No, that
made no sense.

But if she wanted more, if she wanted a passport to a
lifestyle she could never have attained in a million years,
then was it so inconceivable that he give it to her…?

'I don't want to buy you,' he murmured. 'I want to
marry you…'

CHAPTER NINE

'Sorry?' There was a rushing sound in her ears. She thought it might have temporarily impaired her hearing.

'You say you can't be in a relationship if you think it's not going anywhere. Curious considering we embarked on this relationship in the expectation that it wouldn't go anywhere.'

'I didn't think a game of make-believe would…would…' Violet was still grappling with what he had said. Had he actually asked her to marry him? Had she imagined the whole thing? He certainly didn't have the expectant, love struck look of a man who had just voiced a marriage proposal.

'Nor did I. And yet it did and now here we are. Which brings me back to my marriage proposal.'

So, she hadn't been imagining it. And yet nothing in his expression gave any hint that he was talking about anything of import. His eyes were unreadable, his beautiful face coolly speculative. Violet, on the other hand, could feel a burning that began in the pit of her stomach and moved outwards.

Marriage? To Damien Carver? The concept was at once too incredible to believe and yet fiercely seductive. For a few magical seconds, her mind leapfrogged past all the obvious glitches in his wildly unexpected proposal. She was in love with the man who had asked her to marry him! Even when she had been going out with Stu, even though they had occasionally talked about marriage, she had never felt this wonderful surge of pure happiness.

Reality returned and she regretfully left her happy ever after images behind. 'Why would you want to marry me?'

'I'm enjoying what we have. I'm not getting any younger. Yes, at the time we started out on our charade, I had not given a passing thought to settling down, even though I realised that that was what my mother wanted...'

Too hurt by past rejection to go there again...went through Violet's head.

'Now I can see that it makes sense.'

'Makes sense?'

'We get along. You've bonded with my family. They like you. My mother sings your praises. Dominic tells me that you're one of a kind, a gem.' He paused, thought of Annalise with distaste, wondered how he could ever have been so naive as to think that only idiots viewed disability as an unacceptable challenge. He remembered how he had borne the insult delivered to his brother as much as if it had been directly delivered to him. Annalise might have been attractive and clever, but neither of those attributes could have made up for her basic inability to step out of the box. Her neatly laid out future had not included hitches of that nature. Over the years, he had bumped into her, sometimes coincidentally, occasionally at her request. She never mentioned Dominic but she always made a point of informing him how much she had grown up. The fact that Violet naturally and without trying had endeared herself to his mother and his brother counted for a great deal.

'You've asked me to marry you because I get along with your family?'

'Well...that's not the complete story. There's also the

incredible sex…' He scanned her flushed cheeks with lingering appreciation.

'So let me get this straight. You've asked me to marry you because I've been accepted by your family, because we get along and because we're good in bed together. It's not exactly the marriage proposal I dreamed of as a girl.' She kept her voice steady and calm. Inside, her heart was hammering as she absorbed the implications of his proposal. This wasn't about love or a starry-eyed desire to walk off into the sunset with her, holding hands, knowing that they were soulmates, destined to be together for the rest of their lives. This was a marriage proposal of convenience.

'And what when we get tired of one another? I mean, lust doesn't last for ever.' And without love as its foundation, whatever was left when the lust bit disappeared would crumble into dust. When that happened, would he decide that being stuck in a loveless marriage was maybe not quite the sensible option he had gone for? Would his eyes begin to wander? Would he see that other options were available? Of course he would and where would that leave her? Nursing even more heartbreak than if she walked away now with her pride and dignity intact.

'I don't like hypothesising.' Why hadn't she just said yes? He was giving her what any other woman on the planet would want. He knew that without a shred of conceit. He had a lot to offer and he was offering it to her, so what was with the hesitancy and the thousand and one questions? Would he have to fill out an informal questionnaire? To find out if he passed with flying colours?

'I know, but sometimes it's important to look ahead,' Violet persisted stubbornly. In some strange way, this marriage proposal was the nail in the coffin of their relationship. At least as far as she was concerned. She might have wondered aloud where they were going, but she knew, deep down, that she would have been persuaded to carry on, just as she knew that, in carrying on, she would have clung to the belief that her love was returned, that it was just a question of time. She would have allowed hope to propel her forward. But he had proposed what would be a sham of a marriage and she knew, now, exactly where she stood with him.

He liked her well enough but primarily he liked her body. And the added bonus was that she got along with Eleanor and Dominic. When the scales were balanced, he doubtless thought that they weighed in favour of putting a ring on her finger.

'It's not necessary to look ahead,' Damien countered, but sudden unease was stirring a potent mix of anger and bewilderment inside him. 'And I'm not sure where the cross-examination is leading.'

'I can't accept your offer,' Violet said bluntly. 'I'm sorry.'

'Come again?'

'*You* might think we're suited, but I don't.'

'Do we or do we not have amazing sexual chemistry? Do I or do I not turn you on until you're begging me to take you?'

'That's not the point.'

'So you're back to this business of looking for your soulmate. Is that it?'

'There's nothing wrong in thinking that when you settle down you'll do so with the right guy...'

'Do you know the statistics when it comes to divorce? One in three. May even be one in two and a half. For every woman with stars in her eyes and dreams of rocking chairs on verandas with her husband when they're eighty-four with the great-grandchildren running around their feet, I'll show you a hundred who have recently signed their divorce papers and are complaining about the cost of the lawyer's fees. For every child at home with both parents, I'll show you a thousand who have become nomads, travelling between parents and inheriting an assorted family of half-siblings and step-siblings along the way.' He raked impatient, frustrated fingers through his hair. She had made noises about wanting more, and he had blithely assumed that the more she claimed to be wanting was with *him*. It hadn't occurred to him that the more she wanted was with someone else. There was still this amazing, once in a lifetime buzz between them. Was it his fault that he had interpreted that in the only way that seemed possible? And yet here she was, turning him down flat.

'I know that,' Violet said, her mouth stubbornly downturned. Of course, every argument he might use to persuade her that tying the knot was a sensible outcome to their relationship would be based in statistics. In the absence of real emotion, statistics would come in very handy.

She was also aware that sex was only part of the drive behind his proposal. Eleanor's illness had shattered the complacent world he had established around himself and forced him into re-evaluating his relationship with his brother and, by extension, his mother. It had been easy for him to justify his interaction with them and convince himself that there was nothing out of kilter by throwing money in their direction. They had wanted for nothing. Damien had not told her that himself. She had garnered that information via Eleanor, passing remarks, rueful observations... However, as everyone knew, money was not the be-all and end-all when it came to relationships and he had been helped in his fledgling attempts to rebuild what had been lost thanks to her. She knew that without having to be told. She had not entered this peculiar arrangement ever thinking that it would extend beyond the absolutely necessary and yet it had and now all of that had entered the murky mix of logic and rationale that lay behind his proposal.

She didn't want to end up being the convenient other half in a relationship where she would inevitably be taken for granted, nor was it fair on either Eleanor or Dominic for her to slot into their lives where she would eventually pick up the slack, enabling Damien to return to his workaholic life which had no room for anyone, least of all a wife. Even a wife he might temporarily be in lust with.

And yet when she thought of waking up next to him, being able to turn and reach out and touch his warm, responsive body...every morning...

When she half closed her eyes she could recall the feel of his mouth all over her body, kissing and licking and exploring, and a treacherous little voice in her head insisted on telling her that that could be hers. Lust could last a very long time, couldn't it? It could last for ever. It could turn into something else. Couldn't it?

And yet he had approached her the way a person would approach a mathematical equation that needed solving. And that wasn't right. Not when it came to marriage.

But she still had to take a deep breath and steel herself against being sidetracked. Especially when he was sitting right there in front of her, his hands loosely linked, his body leaning towards her, his dark, sinfully beautiful face stirring all sorts of rebellious thoughts inside her.

'But—' she inhaled deeply '—I'm on the side of the minority who actually have working marriages and kids with both parents.' She plucked at her jumper with nerveless fingers. 'And please stop looking at me as though I'm mad. There are some of us out there who prefer to dream rather than just cave in and think that we're never going to be happy...'

'No one's talking about being happy or not being happy…' Damien interrupted impatiently. 'Where did you get that idea from? Did I ask you to marry me with the sub-clause that you shouldn't hold out for happiness?' He wondered why he was continuing to pursue this. She had turned him down and it was time now to take his leave. And yet, although he could feel the sharp teeth of pride kicking in, something was compelling him to stay. Was it because he was keenly aware of how awkward it was going to be breaking the news of their break-up to his mother and Dominic? Made sense. Who liked to be the harbinger of bad news, as he undoubtedly would be? Were it any other woman, he would have left by now. Actually, were it any other woman he would not have proposed in the first place.

'We're not suited. Not in any way that makes sense for a long-term relationship. We might enjoy…you know… the physical side of things…' At this point, she felt faint at that physical side of things no longer being attainable. No more of that breathless excitement. No more melting as their bodies united. But, much more than that, no more heady anticipation knowing that the man she loved was going to be walking through her front door, taking her in his arms… How had she only managed to now work out what should have been obvious from the start? That so much more than just her body looked forward to seeing him? That he had awakened a side to her that she never knew existed and something like that didn't happen in a vacuum? That she just didn't have the sort of personality that could lock away various sides of herself and only bring them out when appropriate?

She had sleep walked herself into loving him and it was a feeling that would never be returned. No amount of persuasive arguments about divorce statistics could change that.

'You're repeating yourself. I don't think there's much point to my remaining here to listen to any more of the same old.' He made to stand and a wave of sickening panic rushed through her at speed, with the force and power of a tsunami.

'But I know you agree with me!' Desperate to keep him with her just a little bit longer, Violet sprang to her feet and placed a restraining hand on his arm.

He looked down at it with withering eyes. 'Our days of touching are over. So…if you don't mind?' He raised one cool eyebrow and Violet removed her hand with alacrity.

'We would end up in a bitter, corrosive relationship if we got married,' she gabbled on, clasping her hands tightly together because she wanted to reach out again and pluck at him to stay. His face was stony. 'I'm sorry I ever said anything about…about… We'd be far better off staying just as we are…' Violet knew that she was backtracking and that there was desperation in that but there was a void opening up in front of her that she knew would be impossible to fill. It was dark and bottomless and terrifying. So what if they just carried on the way they were? Would it be the end of the world? And wouldn't it be better than this? Being a martyr? Hadn't she agreed with him once that martyrdom was cold comfort?

'I don't think so,' Damien said coolly, as he began getting his things together. 'That window's closed, I'm afraid.'

Violet fell back and looked at him in numb silence until he was ready to leave.

'I'll tell my mother this weekend that things didn't work out between us.'

'Let me come with you.' She could feel tears pushing to the back of her eyes.

'What for?'

'I'd like to explain to her myself that…that…'

'There's nothing to explain, Violet. Relationships come and go. Fortunately my mother is in a better place. She'll be able to cope with the disappointment. I wouldn't lose sleep over that if I were you.'

Violet could feel him mentally withdrawing from her at a rate of knots. She hadn't complied and there was no room for anyone in his life who didn't comply.

'Of course I'm going to lose sleep over it! I'm very fond of both Eleanor and Dominic!'

Damien shrugged as though it was of relatively little importance one way or the other. He was moving towards the door. Where was the necklace? No matter. He wanted to tell her that she could consider it a suitable parting gift but he knew he would have to listen to a lecture on all the things money, apparently, couldn't buy. He gritted his teeth at the uncomfortable notion that he would miss those lectures of hers, which had ranged from the ills of money to the misfortune of those who thought they needed it to be happy. She was adept at pointing out all the expensive items that had brought nothing but misery to their owners. She always seemed to have a mental tally at the ready of famous people whose lives had not been improved because they were rich, and had been prone to loftily ignoring him when he pointed out that she should stop reading trashy magazines with celebrity gossip. In between the fantastic sex, which had evolved from their charade in a way that had taken him one hundred per cent by surprise, he was uncomfortably aware that she might have got under his skin in ways he hadn't anticipated.

'In that case,' he returned with supreme indifference, 'I suggest you go see your local friendly doctor and ask him to prescribe you some sleeping pills.'

'How can you be so…so…unsympathetic?' She was traipsing along behind him to the front door. Before she knew it, he was pulling it open, one foot already out as though he couldn't wait to leave her behind.

'There's no point in you having any involvement with me or my family from now on. My mother would be far happier were she spared the tedium of a post-mortem.'

And with that he was gone, slamming the door behind him in a gesture that was as final as the fall of the executioner's axe.

Left on her own, Violet suddenly realised just how lonely the little house was without the promise of his exciting, unsettling presence to bring it to life. She lethargically tidied up the kitchen but her thoughts were exclusively on Damien. She had backed him into a corner and it was no good asking herself whether she had done the right thing or not. You couldn't play around with reality and hope that it might somehow be changed into something else.

But neither could she put thoughts of him behind her as easily as she might have liked. School was no longer gloriously enjoyable because she was busy looking forward to seeing him. There were no little anecdotes saved up for retelling. She spent the following week with the strange sense of having been wrapped up in insulation, something so thick that the outside world seemed to exist around her at a distance. She listened to everyone laughing and chatting but it was all a blur. When Phillipa phoned in a state of high excitement to tell her that she and Andy were getting married at the end of the year, on a beach no less, and would she come over, help her choose a dress or at least a suitably white sarong and bikini, she heard herself saying all the right things but her mind was cloudy, not operating at full whack, as though she had been heavily sedated to the point where her normal reflexes were no longer in proper working order.

Several times she wondered whether she should call Eleanor. But was Damien right? Would his mother be happier to accept their break-up without having to conduct a long conversation about it? Furthermore, what would she say? She had no idea what Damien would have told her. For all she knew, he might have told her that she was entirely to blame, that she had turned into a shrew, a harpy, a gold-digger. It was within his brief to say anything, safe in the knowledge that he wouldn't be contradicted.

And yet she couldn't imagine him being anything other than fair, which, reason told her, was ridiculous, considering the way their relationship had commenced. He had blackmailed her into doing what he wanted. Since when had he turned into a good guy? He had drifted into a sexual relationship for no better reason than she had made a change from the sort of women he usually dated, but he had nothing to offer aside from a consummate ability to make love. So how was it that she had managed to fall in love with him? For every glaring downside in his personality, her rebellious mind insisted on pointing out the good things about him—his wit, his sincere attempts to do what was right for his family, his incredible intellect, which would have made a lesser man sneering and contemptuous of those less gifted than he was, and yet, in Damien's case, did not.

The decision to call Eleanor or not was taken out of her hands when, a week and a half after Damien had walked out of her house, Eleanor called.

She sounded fine. Yes, yes, yes, everything was coming along nicely. The prognosis was good…

'But my son tells me that the two of you have decided to take a break…'

So that was how he had phrased it. Clever in so far as he had left open the possibility that the break might not be permanent. His mother's disappointment would be drip-fed in small stages, protecting her from any dramatic stress their separation might have engendered.

'Um…yes…that's the…er…plan…'

'I confess that I was very surprised indeed when Damien told me…'

'And I'm so sorry I wasn't there to break the news as well, Eleanor.' Violet rushed into apologetic speech. 'I wanted so much to…er…'

'I'd never seen Damien so relaxed and happy.' Eleanor swept past Violet's stammering interruption. 'A different man. I've always worried about the amount of time he devotes to work, but you must have done something wonderful to him, my darling, because he's finally seemed to get his perspective in order… He hasn't just made time for me, but he's made time for his brother…'

'That's…great…'

'Which is why I'm puzzled as to how it is that suddenly you and he are…taking a break…especially when I can see how much the two of you love one another…'

'No! No, no, no… Damien just isn't…he's…we…'

'You're stumbling over your words, my darling,' Eleanor said gently. 'Take your time. You love my son. I know you do. A woman knows these things when it comes to other women…especially an old lady like me…'

Violet lapsed into temporary defeated silence. What could she say to that? Even with Eleanor talking down the end of a phone, she still had the uncanny feeling that the older woman was seeing right into the very heart of her. 'You're not old,' she finally responded. 'And I'm so glad the treatment's going well…'

'Is that your way of changing the conversation?' Eleanor asked tartly. 'Darling, I do wish we could have sat down and talked about this together, woman to woman. Somehow, hearing it from Damien…well, you know what men are like. He can be terribly tight-lipped when it comes to expressing anything emotional…'

'That's true…'

'So why don't you pop over to his place, say this evening…around eight…? We can…chat…'

With unerring ability, Violet realised that Eleanor had found her Achilles heel. She would have thought that Hell might have frozen over before she faced Damien again. She just wanted to somehow try and get him out of her system and paying him a visit was the last thing destined to achieve that goal. But she was very fond of his mother and Eleanor, despite her cheerful optimism about her health, did not deserve to be stressed out.

She was also still in the throes of guilt at not having spoken to the older woman yet.

'You're in London?'

'Flying visit. Check-up… So, darling, I really must dash now. I'll see you shortly, shall I? Can't tell you how much I'm looking forward to that! Don't think that I'm going to allow you to creep out of my life that easily.'

Those two, Eleanor thought with satisfaction as she peered through the window of her chauffeur-driven car on her way back down to Devon, needed to have their heads banged together. Or at least made to sit and really talk because she refused to believe that whatever had taken place between them couldn't be sorted with a heartfelt conversation. And who better to engineer that but herself? If, at the end of it, things were over, then so be it but Damien had been so sketchy in his details, so alarmingly evasive…and men so often didn't recognise what was best for them…

Violet was disconnected before she had time to start thinking on her feet. Was, for instance, Damien going to be present? Would there be an awkward three-way conversation where they both tried desperately to undo what they had so carefully knitted together at the very beginning? She assumed not. She assumed that Eleanor had invited her for a one to one. She had no idea what she would say to the other woman. She would have to be vague. Her fingers itched to dial Damien's mobile and ask him what he had said to his mother but she felt faint just at the thought of hearing that deep, dark, sexy drawl down the end of the line.

Several hours later, standing in front of the imposing Georgian block, some of which had been converted into luxury apartments, others remaining as vast houses, such as his, Violet had to fight down a sickening attack of nerves.

The road where he lived was a statement to the last word in opulence. Gleaming back wrought-iron railings guarded each of the towering white-fronted mansions. The steps to each front door were identical in their scrubbed cleanliness and the front doors were all black with shiny brass knockers for appearance only as a bank of buzzers was located at the side.

She had only been to his place a handful of times but she remembered it clearly. The exquisite hall with its flagstoned floor, the pale walls, the blond wooden flooring that dominated the huge open spaces. Everything within those mega-expensive walls was of the highest standard and state-of-the-art. There was no clutter. She had always found its lack of homeliness off-putting. Now, as she dithered in front of the imposing black door, she had to take some deep breaths to steady her nerves, even though she was nearly a hundred per cent certain that he would not be at home. A cosy chat with Eleanor and she would be on her way. Her uneasy conscience that she hadn't contacted the older woman would be put to rest. They would meet in the future, of course they would, and it would be fine just as long as Damien wasn't around, and maybe, down the line, he could be around because she would have moved on from him.

She pressed the buzzer and settled back to wait because she was certain that Eleanor would not be moving at the speed of light to get to the door, however keen she was to see her.

It had been a lovely day which had mellowed into a cool but pleasant evening. In this expensive part of London, there were few cars and even less foot traffic and she was idly watching a young woman saunter past on the opposite side of the wide, tree-lined road, attempting to infuse a reluctant puppy with enthusiasm for a walk it clearly didn't want, when the door was pulled open behind her.

The greeting died on her lips. For a few seconds her heart seemed to arrest. Damien framed the doorway. He was wearing a pair of faded black jeans that hugged his long, muscular legs and a white T-shirt, close-fitting enough to outline the strong, graceful lines of his body. Memories of touching that body rushed towards her in a tidal wave of hot awareness. In only a matter of a few months, he had guided her down myriad sensual roads never explored before. Her mouth went dry as she thought of a few of them.

'What are you doing here?' she asked inanely.

'It's my house and, funny…I was just about to ask you the same thing.' He half stepped out, pulling the door behind him and blocking out the light from the hall.

'I came to see your mother.' She just wanted to stare and stare and keep on staring. Instead, she looked down at her shoes, some sensible black ballet pumps that worked well with her skinny jeans. She had stopped dressing to hide. It was one of his many lasting legacies to her—the self-confidence to be the person she was.

'And that would be…? Because…?' Damien leant indolently against the doorframe and folded his arms. His fabulous eyes were veiled and watchful as he stared down at her. However, his nerves were taut and he was angry with himself for the seeping away of his self-control. There was nothing left to be said on the subject of their non-relationship. He had offered her marriage. She had thrown his offer back in his face and he was not a man who allowed second bites at the cherry.

He wondered why she had come. Had she had second thoughts? Had she come round to all the advantages marriage to him would provide? His mouth curled with derision. He shifted as his body refused to cooperate and jumped into gear as his eyes unconsciously traced the sexy outline of her breasts underneath the figure-hugging top she was wearing. But hell, she could wear something only seen on someone's maiden aunt and yet have any red-blooded male spinning round in his tracks to stare. He couldn't understand how he could ever have credited her with being anything but sex on legs. He must have been blind and those tight jeans…that jumper. He wanted to pounce and rip them off her so that he could touch what was underneath. Given the circumstances, it was an entirely inappropriate reaction and he was furious with himself for even allowing his mind to travel down those pathways.

'Because your mother phoned and asked me to come here,' Violet muttered. She balled her hands into fists. So he didn't even have the simple courtesy to ask her inside. He would rather conduct a hostile conversation on his doorstep.

'Pull the other one, Violet. My mother left to return to Devon hours ago. So tell me why you imagine she would be waiting here for you? No, don't bother to answer that. I wasn't born yesterday. I *know* what you're doing here.'

Violet's mouth dropped open and she looked at him in bewilderment. At the same time, it was dawning on her that she had been coaxed into coming to his house by Eleanor, who had schemed for…what, exactly? A heartfelt talk where their so-called differences would be ironed out? And a reconciliation might take place? If only she knew the truth of their relationship.

'And you can forget it.'

'Forget what?'

'Any plan you might be concocting to show up here unannounced and resume where we left off.'

'I wasn't doing any such thing!' Violet gasped.

'Expect me to believe that? When you're dressed in the tightest clothes possible? Showing off your assets to maximum advantage?' He pictured her in the unflattering dress she had worn that very first time when she had hesitantly walked into his office and scowled because the image didn't dispel his reaction to her body.

'You're being ridiculous! Your mother asked me over here. She said she wanted to chat and I felt guilty because I should have called her, I should have made contact!'

Damien was fast reaching the same conclusion as Violet had only seconds before. She hadn't come here to try and entice him back into the bedroom. Having recognised that, he had to firmly bank down the fleeting suspicion that he rather enjoyed the notion of her making a pass at him. Naturally, he would have rejected it. But not before he felt immense satisfaction at having her plead with him for a second chance.

'You're impossible!' Violet could scarcely believe the accusations flying at her. Admittedly, there was some small chance that he might have jumped to the wrong conclusions, but how on earth could he think that she had *dressed to impress*? She was suddenly aware of the tightness of her clothes where she hadn't been before. Her breasts were heavy and aching within the constraints of her lacy bra and, as her eyes travelled upwards, doing a reluctant, hateful tour of his impressive body, she could feel herself getting damp between her thighs. She recalled his fingers down there, his mouth sucking and licking until she was writhing for more.

'You have an ego as big as a cruise liner if you imagine that I would come here to…to…make a pass at you! You're the most arrogant man I've ever met!' She longed to inform him, coldly, that she had moved on, but she couldn't bring herself to utter such a whopper.

As she stood there, floundering in front of his assessing eyes, she heard a voice behind him. A woman's voice. Coy and cajoling. For a few seconds she froze and then her eyes widened as the owner of the voice materialised into view.

How on earth could he have dared to accuse her of wearing tight clothes? The leggy brunette with the short, silky bob was clad in white jeans that fitted like a second skin and a small white vest that left very little to the imagination. She was as slender as a reed and Violet could only stare as the brunette sidled up to Damien and slipped her arm through his.

'Aren't you going to introduce us, darling? Though I guess there's no need. You must be Violet…' The pale blue eyes were glacially cold as she stretched out one thin arm in greeting. 'I'm Annalise…'

CHAPTER TEN

IT WAS RAINING by the time Violet made it back to her house. A fine, needle-sharp drizzle that she barely noticed. She took the Tube and bus back to her house on autopilot. She couldn't think straight and her heart was thumping like a steam engine inside her chest, making it uncomfortable to breathe.

She wanted to block out images of Damien with Annalise. She tried hard to tell herself that it didn't matter, that he was a free man who could do whatever he liked with whomever he liked. Unfortunately, no amount of cool logic could paper over the devastation she felt nor could it stop the flood of painful speculation that assailed her, wave upon wave, upon wave until she wanted to pass out.

He was back with his ex, back with the only woman he had never been able to forget, the only woman to whom he had wanted to commit, fully and without reservation or a list of sensible reasons why the match could work out. It certainly hadn't taken him long to reconnect. Was it because her rejection of his proposal had put things into perspective for him? Made him wake up and realise that marriage was more than a list of dos and don'ts? Had that propelled him to seek out Annalise? Had it reminded him that, in his carefully controlled world, there was still one woman who had broken through the boundaries and that he needed to find her and tell her? They certainly had looked very cosy with one another.

And Annalise was much more his style than she, Violet, could ever hope to be. Tall, skinny, beautiful. Nor did she look like a typical bimbo. No, she looked like one of those rare, annoying breeds—a true beauty who also had brains.

She couldn't look at herself in the mirror as she banged about in the bathroom, getting ready for bed. She didn't want to see the comparisons between her and his ex. Thinking about comparisons drained her of all her self-confidence. Had he only really seen her as a novelty? The broad bean versus the runner bean? Had he fallen into bed with her because she had been *there*? Available and eager? Was he any different from any other man in a situation where opportunity was handed to him on a plate? No one could accuse him of being the sort of guy who took relationships seriously, who held out for the right woman. He was a red-blooded male with a rampant libido who took what he wanted. And she had been there for the taking. And then he had proposed because it was convenient. He was never going to fall in love; he had done that with Annalise, so why not hitch up with the woman who had won his family's approval? Noticeably, he had only proposed when he had woken up to the reality that she might walk out on him.

She climbed into bed and tried to read and only realised that she had actually fallen asleep when she was awakened by two things.

The first was the sound of the rain. It had progressed from a persistent drizzle to the wild rapping of rain against her windows. She had left one window slightly ajar and the voile curtain was blowing furiously under the force of the wind. When she went to close it, she realised that the chest of drawers just underneath was splattered in rainwater but she had no intention of doing anything about that just at the moment.

Because, competing with the howling of the wind and the rain, was the thunderous sound of someone banging on her front door.

Outside, dripping water, Damien was cursing the English weather. Between eight, when he had opened his front door to Violet, and midnight, when he had finally managed to get rid of Annalise, the rain had picked up. Now, at a little after three-thirty, the only thing that could be said in favour of his jumping in his car and coming here was the fact that the roads had been traffic-free.

He noticed that one of the lights in the house had now been turned on and breathed a sigh of relief. He really didn't want to remain outside her house for the remainder of the night, although he would have, had she not answered the door.

Violet had stuck on her bathrobe to see who was at the door. Her immediate thought when she had heard the banging was to imagine that it was someone trying to break in but, almost as soon as she thought that, she realised that it was a ridiculous supposition because since when did intruders give advance notice of their intention by banging on doors?

So was it someone who needed help? She knew her neighbours. The old lady living next door was quite frail. Was there something wrong? She tried and failed to imagine small Mrs Wilson, in her late eighties, having the strength to venture out of her house in the early hours of the morning to bang on a door.

As she hurried downstairs, switching on lights in her wake, she could feel her heart pounding because, of course, there was someone else it might be, but, like her scenario involving the polite burglar knocking to warn her of his imminent break-in, the thought that it might be Damien was too far-fetched to be worth consideration.

The safety chain was on and as she opened the door a crack she knew instantly that the one man she had least expected was standing outside. There was a storm raging outside her house, or so it seemed. The wind was sending his trench coat in all directions and the rain was whipping down at a slant. His feet were planted squarely on the ground but, as she pulled the door open a little wider, he placed his hand against the doorframe to look down at her.

He was drenched. Soaked through.

'What do you want?' Violet wrapped the robe tightly around her. 'What are you doing here?'

'Violet, let me in.'

'Where's your girlfriend, Damien? Is she waiting in the car for you?' She could have kicked herself for mentioning Annalise but, at this point, she really didn't care.

'Let me in.'

'I don't know why you've come but I don't want you here.'

'Please.'

That single word stopped Violet in her tracks. She could feel the rain beating down towards her and she stepped back into the house to avoid being soaked.

'I have nothing to say to you.'

'Maybe there are things that *I* need to say to you.'

But, tellingly, he hadn't followed her into the hall. He remained standing on the doorstep, getting drenched. Was he *hesitant*? Violet thought in some confusion. Surely not! Hesitancy was one of those emotions he didn't do. Along with love. And yet he was still standing there, getting wet and looking at her.

'What could you possibly want to say to me, Damien? I just came to see your mother. I didn't come to try and start back what we had! You're out of my life and if I was a little…a little…disconcerted, it was because I hadn't expected to be confronted with your girlfriend! Quick work, Damien!'

'Ex. Ex-girlfriend. Please let me in, Violet. I'm not going to barge my way into your house and if you tell me that you don't want to see me again, then I'll go.'

Tell him to go and she would never see him again. Of course, that would be for the best. They really had nothing to say to one another. Less than nothing. Maybe he had braved the foul weather because he felt badly, because he wanted to explain to her, face to face, how it was that Annalise was back in his life. Perhaps he thought that he might be doing her a favour by playing the good guy and filling her in. And still, painful though that thought was, her mind seized up when she thought of him disappearing back into the driving rain and vanishing out of her life for good, without saying what he had to say.

'It's late.' She stood aside and folded her arms as he dripped his way into her hall and removed the trench coat. His hair was plastered down and he raked his fingers through it, which just scattered the drops of water.

'Perhaps I could have a towel…'

'I suppose so,' Violet muttered a little ungraciously.

She returned a few minutes later to find him in the same spot, standing in the hall. Where was the guy who had never hesitated to make himself at home? Where was the self-assured man who knew the layout of her kitchen, who might be expected to make himself a cup of coffee?

She watched in silence as he roughly dried himself. He made no attempt to remove his jumper, which clung to him, and she bit back the temptation to tell him to take it off because if he didn't he would catch cold.

'I'm sorry you had to find Annalise in my house,' Damien said heavily.

Violet broke eye contact and headed towards the kitchen. He might be comfortable having a conversation neither of them wanted in the middle of her hallway, but she needed to sit down and she needed something to do with her hands. She was aware of him following her. It might be after three in the morning but every sense in her was on red alert.

'It was unexpected, that's all.' She busied herself with the kettle, mugs, spoons, keeping her back to him because she was scared that if he saw her face he would be able to read what was going on in her mind. 'Like I said…'

'I know. My mother got you there on false pretences. I spoke to her. She…thought that a little bit of undercover matchmaking wouldn't go amiss…'

'And did you tell her about Annalise?'

'No. There *is* no Annalise.'

And he didn't know what had possessed him to open the door to her when she had showed up the previous evening. He had opened the door and he had invited her in. She had heard about Violet. Friend of a friend of a friend had seen them together at a restaurant…there were rumours…gossip, even…she was curious…he could talk to *her*…after all, they had a history…they were connected… weren't they…?

At that point, Damien knew that he should have escorted her out. It was quite different bumping into her at a random company affair or even occasionally meeting her in a public place where, like a masochist, he could be reminded of his narrow escape, but letting her into his house had not been a good idea.

And yet hadn't there been a part of him that had *questioned* whether Annalise might not be reintroduced into his life? Violet had walked out and he hadn't known what to do with the chaos of his emotions when she had left. Hadn't a part of him bitterly wondered whether Annalise, who could never wield the sort of crazy control over him that Violet had, might not just be the better bet? He had had his marriage proposal chucked back in his face. Annalise…well, he could buy her and what you could buy, you could control.

He had let her in and the moment of questioning had gone as quickly as it had arrived. But she was in his house and, foolishly, he had prevaricated about throwing her out. Would it have been asking too much of fate to step aside for a while and not steer Violet towards his doorstep?

'What do you mean?' Clasping her cup of coffee between her hands, she stalked out towards the sitting room. She hadn't offered him anything to drink. It was meant as a pointed reminder that she had only allowed him in under duress, but really, if he thought that he could somehow try and come up smelling of roses, then he was mistaken.

She sat down and when she looked up it was to find him hovering by the door.

'You might as well sit down, Damien. But I'm tired and I'm not in the mood for a conversation.'

'I know.' He removed the jumper, which was heavy and wet, and carefully put it over one of the radiators, then he prowled over to the window, parted the curtains a crack and peered outside into the bleak rainy night. 'I didn't invite her,' he offered at last. 'She showed up.'

'It's none of my business anyway.'

'Everything I do should be your business,' Damien muttered, flushing darkly. 'At least, that's what I'd like.' He thought that this must be what it felt like to indulge in a dangerous sport, one where the outcome was a life or death situation. 'And I would understand if you don't believe me, Violet.'

'I don't understand what you're saying.' Violet's voice was wary. She couldn't tear her eyes away from him. He was even more compelling in this strangely vulnerable, puzzling mood. It was a side to him she had never seen before and it threw her. He circled the room, one hand in his trouser pocket, the other playing with his hair, before finally standing directly in front of her so that she was forced to look up at him.

'Would you mind sitting down? I'm getting a crick in my neck looking up at you.'

'I need you to sit next to me,' Damien told her roughly. 'There are things I need...to say to you and I need to have you...next to me when I say them...' He sat on the sofa and patted the spot next to him. 'Please, Violet.' He grinned crookedly and looked away. 'I bet you've never heard me say *please* so many times.'

'I can't do this. Just tell me why you've come. You didn't have to. I know we had...something. You probably feel obliged to explain yourself to me. Well, don't. So we broke up and you've returned to the love of your life.' Violet shrugged. The vacant space on the sofa next to him begged her to fill it but she wasn't going to give in to that dangerous temptation. He had this effect on her...could make her take her eyes off the ball and she wasn't going to fall victim to that now.

'I told you Annalise was my ex and she still is.'

'And this is the ex you've seen on and off over the years?'

'Sometimes it pays to be reminded of your mistakes.'

'I beg your pardon?'

'I can't talk when you're sitting on the other side of the room. It's hard enough...as it is... I don't usually...'

He raked his fingers through his hair and realised that he was shaking.

Reluctantly, Violet went to perch on the sofa. Just closing this small gap between them made her stomach twist in nervous knots.

'Once upon a time,' Damien said heavily, 'I fancied myself in love with Annalise. I was young. She was beautiful, clever…ticked all the boxes. It was a whirlwind romance, just the sort of thing you read about in books, and I proposed to her.'

'You don't need to tell me any of this,' Violet interjected stiffly and yet she wanted to hear every word of it.

'I need to and I want to. You'd be surprised if I told you that I've never felt the slightest inclination to share any of the details of my relationship with Annalise with anyone.'

'I wouldn't be surprised. You keep everything locked up inside.'

'I do.'

'You're agreeing with me. Why?'

'Because you're right. I've always kept everything locked up inside. It's why no one has ever known what Annalise really meant to me.'

And he was about to tell her. Yet the details so far weren't adding up to the love of his life and she fought to subdue the tendril of hope unfurling inside her that there might be another side of the story. Ever since she had met him, her placid life had become a roller coaster ride, hope alternating with despair before rising again to the surface like a terrible virus over which she had no control. Did she want to get back on that ride? Did she want to nurture that tendril of hope until it began growing into something uncontrollable? She could feel tears of frustration and dismay prick the back of her eyes. She curled her fingers in her lap and was shocked when he reached out and slowly un-curled them so that he could abstractedly play with them.

It was just the lightest of touches but it was enough to send her body into wild shock.

'Annalise turned me down because she couldn't cope with the prospect of being saddled, at some point in time, with a disabled brother-in-law.'

'What?' This was not what she had been expecting to hear and she leaned forward to catch what he was saying.

'She met Dominic and I knew instantly that she couldn't cope with his condition. For Annalise, everything was about perfection. Dominic was not perfect. She knew that at some point I would be responsible for him. She had vi-sions of him living with us, her having to incorporate him into the perfect world she was desperate to have.'

'That's...that's awful...' Violet reached out and rested her hand on his arm and felt him shudder.

'From that moment onwards, I knew that never again would I put myself in a position of vulnerability. I enjoyed women but they had their place and I made damn sure that they never overstepped it. And just in case I was ever tempted to forget, I made sure that Annalise was never completely eliminated from my life.'

'And yet she was there tonight. In your...in your house...'

'You turned me down. I asked you to marry me and you turned me down.'

Because you couldn't love me! Despite everything he had said, he still didn't love her. He was just explaining why he couldn't. She would do well to remember that and not get swept away by this strange mood he was in and his haltering confidences.

'When Annalise showed up on my doorstep, I let her in because I was...not myself. No, that doesn't really explain it either. I was going out of my mind. Had been ever since we broke up. I told myself that it was for the best, that you could damn well go your own way and find out first-hand that there was no such thing as the perfect soulmate, but I couldn't think straight, couldn't function… I resented the fact that even when you were no longer around, you were still managing to control my behaviour.'

Violet was finding it impossible to filter the things he was telling her.

'I am ashamed to say that I briefly considered Annalise a known quantity and that maybe the devil you know… Of course, it was just a passing aberration. I got rid of her as fast as I could and then I waited…for normality to return. It didn't.'

'So you came here…to tell me what? Exactly?' She pinned her mouth into a stubborn line but she had broken out in a fine film of nervous perspiration. She tried to ignore the way he was still toying distractedly with her fingers and the way their bodies were leaning urgently towards each other, radiating a fevered heat that made her want to swoon. His familiar scent filled her nostrils. Once, she had found him devastatingly attractive. Having slept with him, knowing the contours of his lean, hard body, the body along which she had run her hands and her mouth so many times, made him horribly, painfully irresistible. Familiarity hadn't bred contempt. The opposite. It had ratcheted up the level of his sexual pull to the extent that she could barely think of anything else as she continued to stare at him, pupils dilated, dreading the way her body was reacting in ways her brain was telling it not to.

'That I proposed to you because…it made sense. I didn't realise…' He withdrew his hand to tousle his dark hair. 'I didn't think that I might have needed you in my life for reasons that didn't make any sense. That you'd climbed under my skin and it wasn't just to do with the good sex.'

'What was it to do with?'

'I'm in love with you. I don't know when that happened or how, but…'

'Say that again?'

'Which bit?'

'The bit about being in love with me.' A feeling of being on top of the world, of pure joy, filled her like life-saving oxygen. She felt heady and giddy and euphoric all at the same time. 'You didn't say,' she told him accusingly, but she was half laughing, half wanting to cry. 'Why didn't you say?'

'I didn't know…until you left…'

She flung herself into his arms and sighed with pure contentment when he wrapped his arms around her and held her close, so close that she could hear the beating of his heart. 'You were so arrogant,' she told him. 'You forced me into an arrangement I hated. You broke all the rules when it came to the sort of guy I could ever be interested in. You didn't want any kind of long-term relationship and I've never approved of men who move from woman to woman. And, as well, I was convinced that you were still wrapped up with Annalise, that you'd never let the memory go, that she was the ex no one had ever been able to live up to. On all fronts you were taboo, and then I met your family and I got sucked in to you…to all of you…and it was like being in quicksand. When you proposed, when you listed all the reasons why marrying me would make sense, I finally woke up to the fact that the one reason why anyone should get married was missing. You didn't love me. I thought you didn't know how and you never would and I couldn't accept your offer, knowing that the power balance would be so uneven. I would forever be the helpless, dependent one, madly in love with you and waiting for the time when you got tired of me physically and the axe fell.'

'And now?'

'And now I'm the happiest person in the world!'

'So if I ask you again to marry me…this time for all the right reasons…'

'Yes! Yes! Yes!'

Damien shuddered with relief. He felt as if he'd been holding his breath ever since he'd walked into the house. His arms tightened around her and he breathed in the fresh floral smell of her hair. 'You've made me the happiest person in the world as well…' Then he gave a low rumble of laughter. 'And I don't think my mother or Dominic will mind too much either…'

EPILOGUE

THEY DIDN'T MIND. Not when Damien and Violet showed up, surprising both Dominic and Eleanor, the following day.

'Of course,' Eleanor said smugly, 'I knew it was just a case of getting you two together so that you could sort out your silly differences. Damien, darling, I love you but you can be stubborn and there was no way that I was going to allow the best thing that ever happened to you to slip through your fingers. Now, let's discuss the wedding plans… Something big and fancy? Or small and cosy…?'

'Fast,' was Damien's response.

They were married six weeks later at the local church close to his mother's house. Dominic was the best man and he performed his duties with a gravity that was incredibly touching and, later, at the small reception which they held at the house, he was cheered on to speak and, bright red, raised his glass to the best brother a man could have.

Phillipa didn't stop teasing her sister that she had managed to beat her down the aisle. 'And you'll probably be preggers by the time I make my vows in my white sarong and crop top!' she wailed, which, as it turned out, was exactly what happened.

On a hot day, watching her sister and her assortment of new-found friends, with the sound of the surf competing with the little band drumming out the wedding march as

Phillipa took her vows, Violet leaned against her husband, hand on the gentle swell of her stomach, and wondered whether it was possible to be happier.

From those inauspicious beginnings, the relationship she never thought would happen had blossomed into something she could not live without, and the man who had fought against becoming involved had turned into the man who frequently told her how much he loved her and how much he hated leaving her side.

'I've come to terms with the value of delegation,' he had confided without a shade of regret, 'and when my son is born...'

'Or daughter...'

'*Or daughter*...I intend to explore its value even more...'

Thinking about what else they explored now brought a hectic flush to her cheeks and, as if reading her mind, Damien leant to whisper in her ear, 'Okay. The ceremony is over. What do you say to us staying for the meal and then heading back to the hotel? I think I need to remind myself of what your nipples taste like... I'm getting withdrawal symptoms...'

Violet blushed and laughed and looked up at him. 'That would be rude...' she said sternly, but already her mind was leaping ahead to the way her developing body fascinated him, the way he lavished attention on her breasts, even more abundant now, and suckled on her nipples, which were bigger and darker and a source of never-ending attention the minute her clothes were off. She felt the heat pool between her legs when she thought of them lying in the air-conditioned splendour of their massive curtained bed, his head on her stomach while he stroked her thighs with his hand, then tickled the swollen, engorged bud of her clitoris, which she would swear was even more sensitive now.

'But I'm sure Phillipa will understand...' she conceded as he planted a fleeting kiss on the corner of her mouth. 'After all, we pregnant ladies can't stay in the heat for too long...'

* * * * *

COMING NEXT MONTH FROM
HARLEQUIN *Presents*

Available January 21, 2014

#3209 A BARGAIN WITH THE ENEMY
The Devilish D'Angelos
Carole Mortimer

International tycoon Gabriel D'Angelo is haunted by the unforgiving eyes that once stared at him across a crowded courtroom. Now the enticing Bryn Jones is back, and this time he'll ensure she plays by *his* rules to get what she wants....

#3210 SHAMED IN THE SANDS
Desert Men of Qurhah
Sharon Kendrick

Bound by a life of restrictions and rules, Princess Leila is desperate for freedom—and Gabe Steel holds the key. Enthralled by her intoxicating touch, Gabe doesn't realize her royal connection...or the lengths he'll have to go to protect her from shame!

#3211 WHEN FALCONE'S WORLD STOPS TURNING
Blood Brothers
Abby Green

Rafaele Falcone may have walked away from her years before, and his sexy Italian accent might still send shivers down her spine, but Samantha Rourke is in the driver's seat this time...with the power to change everything for the ruthless tycoon.

#3212 SECURING THE GREEK'S LEGACY
Julia James

To secure his family's empire, Anatole Telonides must get the beautiful Lyn Brandon to agree to his command...but Lyn is more than the shrinking violet she seems. Her steely resistance entices him to make the ultimate sacrifice—marriage!

HPCNM0114RB

REQUEST YOUR
FREE BOOKS!

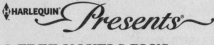

2 FREE NOVELS PLUS
2 FREE GIFTS!

YES! Please send me 2 FREE Harlequin Presents® novels and my 2 FREE gifts (gifts are worth about $10). After receiving them, if I don't wish to receive any more books, I can return the shipping statement marked "cancel." If I don't cancel, I will receive 6 brand-new novels every month and be billed just $4.30 per book in the U.S. or $4.99 per book in Canada. That's a saving of at least 14% off the cover price! It's quite a bargain! Shipping and handling is just 50¢ per book in the U.S. and 75¢ per book in Canada.* I understand that accepting the 2 free books and gifts places me under no obligation to buy anything. I can always return a shipment and cancel at any time. Even if I never buy another book, the two free books and gifts are mine to keep forever.

106/306 HDN FVRK

Name	(PLEASE PRINT)	
Address		Apt. #
City	State/Prov.	Zip/Postal Code

Signature (if under 18, a parent or guardian must sign)

Mail to the **Harlequin® Reader Service:**
IN U.S.A.: P.O. Box 1867, Buffalo, NY 14240-1867
IN CANADA: P.O. Box 609, Fort Erie, Ontario L2A 5X3

**Are you a current subscriber to Harlequin Presents books
and want to receive the larger-print edition?
Call 1-800-873-8635 or visit www.ReaderService.com.**